I0663688

FAMILY ON FIRE

A MYSTERY THRILLER

DARKNESS MYSTERY SERIES
BOOK SIX

MICHELLE FILES

Edited by
CECILY BROOKES
Edited by
THEAUTHORFILES.COM

INTRODUCTION

Nathan, a devoted father of two, gets the shock of his life when he wakes one morning to find that both of his children are missing.

When they don't return, his world is turned upside down as he is forced to defend himself from accusations and mistrust. The sheriff thinks he did the unthinkable. His relatives don't believe him. His world begins to slowly fall apart.

To find the answers, Nathan must finally come to terms with deep secrets and deceit in his past before he can face the unbelievable truth about his family—and himself.

This fast paced, mystery, suspense novel will keep you turning the pages.

Novels by Michelle Files:

TYLER MYSTERY SERIES:
Girl Lost
A Reckless Life

WILDFLOWER MYSTERY SERIES
Secrets of Wildflower Island
Desperation on Wildflower Island
Storm on Wildflower Island
Thorns on Wildflower Island

IVY WELLS MYSTERY SERIES
The Many Lives of Ivy Wells
The Many Lives of Sam Wells
The Many Lives of Jack Wells
The Many Lives of Georgie Wells

STONE MOUNTAIN FAMILY SAGA
Winters Legend on Stone Mountain
A Dangerous Game on Stone Mountain
Deceit on Stone Mountain

DARKNESS MYSTERY SERIES
Escape the Dark
The Dark Years
The Children
Suspicions on River Road
Sapphire Valley
Family on Fire

For information on any of Michelle's books:
www.MichelleFiles.com

CHAPTER 1

Creeping along the outer walls of the cabin, a dark, dense fog seemed to hug the rough logs, deep, deep in the woods. No one has laid eyes on the cabin in well over two decades. A steady drizzle seemed to envelope the place, giving it an eerie glow from the moonlight.

The girl, drifting between sleep and consciousness, moved only slightly, wincing from the pain. Her skull began to pound. For just a moment, she panicked, wondering where she was. Her eyes fluttered open, but the cabin was pitch dark, and she drew in a quick breath. Reaching out, she could only feel the thick air in front of her.

Struggling to remember where she was, a moment later it came to her.

The cabin in the woods.

It was cold. So very cold. The girl was soaked from head to toe. Shivering, her teeth clanked together, the clacking reverberating off the walls of the mostly empty place. And it was so dark that for a moment she feared she had gone blind.

After a few moments, her eyes started to adjust to the darkness, but she didn't need to look down to know that her feet were bare. Her clothing consisted of only a thin summer, strappy dress. Certainly not even close to enough to keep her warm in the middle of the night.

A noise came from somewhere she couldn't see. She looked toward the single window in the small room. There was only a tiny bit of light. Really not enough to see anything.

A flash across the window. Muffled voices outside. She tried to make herself smaller, as she sat in the corner of the small room in the tiny cabin, underneath a scratchy, thread-bare wool blanket.

The voices were getting closer. Was that a flashlight pointed at the broken window, she wondered.

The drizzle outside made the flashes of light sparkle. The girl almost smiled.

The girl held her breath and her eyes darted to the door-knob, as someone jiggled it. As the door creaked open, she whimpered.

CHAPTER 2

Slowly gaining consciousness, Nathan Ford opened one eye slowly. He squinted in the bright sunlight that seemed to be focusing a beam squarely onto his face. Squeezing his eye shut, he reached up his hand to block out the offending pierce of light.

"Why is that damn window open?" The words were scratchy against his parched throat, and he cleared it as he reached around for something to drink. His hand clanked against something. He could hear the clink of the aluminum can as it bounced off the table, hit the wooden sideboard of his bed and tumbled to the ground. With his eyes still closed, he knew that was the remaining contents of the beer he was drinking when he passed out sometime late the night before.

He tried to lift his head off of the pillow so that he could close the blinds. A brain splitting headache pierced through his skull. Squeezing his eyes even tighter, he tried to will the pain away. It wasn't working. Though he had just awakened, he wanted nothing more than some whiskey and a nap. Maybe the beer would do. He rolled onto his side and reached down toward the floor for the wayward can. Perhaps there was a swallow or two still in the can of beer currently soaking into his bedroom carpet.

But his stomach had other ideas.

Lunging for the bathroom, he made it just in time. His dinner from the night before heaved its way out of him. Nathan stumbled back to his bed and fell into it. The springs groaned in protest.

"I'm never drinking again," he mumbled.

He knew that it was a lie even as the words escaped is mouth.

Grumbling at the still open blinds, he rolled over and buried his face into his pillow. It took Nathan another ten minutes before he managed to get himself into a seated position. At least the spike that seemed to be piercing his brain was mellowing out. Still foggy headed, he glanced over at the red numbers on the clock radio. 11:08 a.m.

Figuring he should probably get up and see what his kids were up to, and if they've had anything to eat that morning, he pulled himself to his feet. At only 40 years old, he knew that his body shouldn't be such a mess. But he wasn't a stupid man. He owned every last bit of blame for that one. His near-constant drinking had ended his marriage, and would probably end his life prematurely. That was something he lived with every day.

Shuffling toward the kitchen in only his boxers and bare feet, Nathan rubbed at his scratchy eyes. He didn't need a mirror to know that they were bloodshot red.

Neither of his children were in the kitchen. He stood and stared at the table while running his fingers through his thick head of salt and pepper hair.

"Ariel, Sean, where are you guys?!" Nathan called.

No response.

"Well, that's weird." Nathan had a penchant for talking to himself.

"Kids! Where is everyone?!"

Still nothing.

"Great. Wait, what day is it?" He found the date on the calendar that was tacked to the refrigerator with a souvenir Grand Canyon magnet. "Saturday." He looked again at the calendar. Nothing was written on it. No outings, no soccer games, no notes, nothing.

"Okay, they gotta be around here somewhere."

Nathan stuck his head out the back door. No kids playing. At 13, his daughter was unlikely to be out playing anyway. She would almost definitely be in her room, on the phone.

He headed for their bedrooms, passing through the dead silent living room. That room was almost never silent. The television seemed to be on 24 hours a day. It was something that drove him nuts, but the kids had it on from waking to bed, every single day.

He checked Sean's room first. He wasn't in his room. His bed appeared to have been slept in, but Nathan couldn't be sure, as Sean never made his bed.

No pajamas graced the floor. That was strange. Sean always left his pajamas right where he changed out of them. Where would he have gone that he would still be wearing them? Nathan checked his son's hamper just to be sure. He dug through the few items of clothing that had actually made their way in, without finding the pajamas.

Other than the missing pajamas, Sean's room looked exactly like it always did. Everything in a bit of disarray. Nothing really looked like it had a place. Even the posters on the wall were crooked. Nathan had tried to help, but 9 year old Sean had insisted that he could do it himself. And he was proud of the job he did. Nathan hadn't the heart to tell him otherwise.

Ariel's room was next. Surely, she would be in there, and

know where Sean went. He was probably up the street, at a friend's house.

Nathan knew better than to just walk into his daughter's bedroom, unannounced. He had been yelled at enough times and learned his lesson. He knocked. Nothing. He knocked again.

"Hey, Ariel, are you in there?"

No answer.

He turned the knob and peered in, knocking as he did so. "Knock knock, hello?"

With no sign of her, he opened the door wider, to get a better look.

She was not in her room either. He couldn't be sure if her bed had been slept in, as she was meticulous about making it every morning.

So where were his children?

Nathan headed back to the kitchen and lifted the yellow telephone receiver off the wall. Sure, he had a cell phone, but still liked having the one central phone in the house, that was always where it should be. He seemed to have a terrible time of keeping track of his phone.

He dialed Ariel's cell phone.

It rang and rang, finally the voicemail picked up. He left a message, knowing that she would never listen to it. She would either call him back, or more likely, text him back.

"Ariel, it's like eleven thirty, and I have no idea where you and Sean are. Can you please call me back asap?"

He put the phone back in its cradle and went searching for his cell phone. If his daughter did text him back, he would need to have it handy. After a ten minute search, he found it underneath his pants lying on the floor at the foot of the bed. He had no recollection of how it got there. Or how his pants got there, for that matter.

There were no calls and no texts from Ariel.

Nathan found his address book on the desk in the kitchen. Yeah, he knew he was old fashioned. No one used actual address books anymore. Except him. Leafing through it, he found the phone number for Sean's two best friends. The three boys were inseparable. Rarely did you see one out in the neighborhood without the other two. Nathan called both of them.

Neither one had seen or talked to him that day.

Now he was officially worried.

Taking no more than a two minute shower and throwing on his shoes, some shorts, and a t-shirt while still damp, and he was out the door in under six minutes. He drove through his Black River neighborhood, searching for his children. He stopped at the houses of the friends he knew. Friends that he had known for years. Not a single kid or parent had heard from either of his children since the day before.

Nathan even stopped in at the convenience store a few blocks away. Nine year old Sean had been known to head that way to stock up on sweets now and then.

Visions of the Black River Killer danced in his head. But the killer had been caught. So there was that. However, Black River was still one of those towns. They continued to have more than their fair share of murders. Not being able to find his children terrified him.

What if….? He stopped. He couldn't let himself go there. Putting any foul play out of his mind, he focused on his search.

After having absolutely no luck in locating either one of the children, Nathan headed home, hoping they would be there when he arrived.

"Is anyone home?" he called as he entered the house. "Come on, anyone? Stop fooling around, guys, I'm starting to worry."

He knew his pleas were pointless. No one was there. The home was eerily silent.

Nathan hesitated before calling the police. But there was no other choice. He needed to call them. It was completely unlike his children to just up and disappear. He cringed at that word. It was something he had been living with for over a year now.

His stomach needed some sustenance. It felt icky and empty at the same time. He grabbed a roll left over from the previous night's dinner and jammed it into his mouth while he dialed.

"Nine-one-one. What is your emergency?" the female voice on the other line asked.

"Um, I can't find my kids anywhere. Please, I need some help."

CHAPTER 3

Deputy Alicia Jones got the call and grabbed her car keys. "Sheriff, I'm heading over to see about a couple of missing kids," she called across the station while heading for the door.

"Hey Jones," Sheriff Garcia called back across the station, "take Cavanaugh here with you."

She looked up at the new face. He was younger than her by not more than four or five years. He was standing in the sheriff's office and the two of them were shaking hands.

Both of them exited the sheriff's office and headed her way. "Jones, this here is Jake Cavanaugh. He is starting with us today."

She reached out her hand and he took it. "Cavanaugh? Why does that sound so familiar...?" Her mind searched for an answer as her voice trailed off. He even looked familiar, but she couldn't quite place him. That's when it hit her. The news. His family had been on the news.

"Oh." Was all she could manage to say.

Sheriff Garcia and the new deputy looked at each other.

They knew this was not going to be an easy transition for Jake.

"Yes Jones, he's the son of the Black River Killer. But we can't rightly blame him for something his mother did, now can we?" The look on the sheriff's face told her that she had better agree, and that she had better be nice to him. Not that she would be anything but nice. Alicia Jones liked everyone… until they gave her a reason not to.

Deputy Jones looked back over at the young man. "No, I suppose not. I'm sorry about my reaction. I was just surprised, that's all."

Jake shook his head. "It's perfectly all right, really. I'm used to it." His smile put her at ease.

The pair drove through the sunny streets of Black River. It was the middle of summer and the days were hot. It was a familiar sight to see children running and screeching through a sprinkler attached to their water hose. Jake smiled.

He and Deputy Alicia Jones didn't speak much on the way over to the Ford residence. He knew how his presence made some people uncomfortable. How do you have a conversation with the son of the most notorious serial killer in Black River history? Hell, in the whole state's history. He knew that many people just didn't know what to say to him. So they said nothing.

Alicia Jones was no different. She tried to make small talk, but it was a disaster. She couldn't figure out how to make the sunny summer weather sound interesting. So she kept her mouth shut. In that small car, with just the two of them present, the silence was deafening.

A few minutes later, to the relief of Deputy Jones, the car made the final turn onto Hill Street. Jones pulled the car along the curb in front of the Ford residence. Jake paused for only a moment as he peered into the back window of a dark green sedan in the driveway. Alicia's stride never wavered, continuing up the sidewalk toward the front door. Jake placed his hand on the hood of the car as he rounded the front of it. He said nothing, and continued moving.

Alicia leaned in toward Jake as he made his way to stand next to her. "What were you doing?" she whispered.

He shrugged. Both turned as Nathan opened his front door before they deputies had a chance to knock.

"Hi, please come in." He opened the door wide and stepped to the side.

They took in his disheveled appearance and bread crumbs in the stubble on his face. Nathan hadn't taken the time to comb his hair after his brief shower. Having only taken a moment to run his fingers through it, then throwing on his t-shirt, his hair now stuck out in several directions. He hadn't noticed, and didn't care.

His living room wasn't in much better shape. It was what Jake's mother used to call "lived in." There were magazines lying on the couch, as well as the coffee table. One had even managed to make its way to the floor, and clearly had been stepped on multiple times. It made Jake wonder how long it had been there and why no one bothered to pick it up.

Someone's left over dinner was on top of one of the magazines, with ants already making a feast out of it. The television and lamps were dusty. It definitely looked like a family who didn't care that it wasn't 'show ready' at all times.

The item that drew the attention of both deputies, however, was the empty bottle of Jameson lying on the table next to the chair. It was dangling precariously over the edge of the table and looked to be bone dry.

"Hello, Mr. Ford. I'm Deputy Jones and this is Deputy Cavanaugh."

"Hi, thank you for coming. I can't find my kids anywhere." Nathan scratched at the stubble on his face. He hadn't taken the time to shave that morning either. "Do you want to sit?"

He motioned toward the plaid brown couch and the clashing chair next to it. The chair was purple and orange, in some sort of swirling pattern. Jake couldn't imagine that anyone bought the pieces of furniture on purpose.

"Uh no, we're good," Jake responded.

"Please give us a bit of information." Jones pulled a notebook and pen from her pocket. "What are your kids' names and ages?"

"My daughter's name is Ariel and she's thirteen. Sean is my nine year old son."

"When did you see them last, Mr. Ford?" Jake asked.

"I just woke up and they were gone." He shrugged.

"Okay. We are going to need more information than that. Did you see them when they went to bed? Or was it sometime earlier than that?" Jake prodded. "Did you check on them sometime during the night?"

Nathan shuffled from foot to foot. "No, none of that. It was sometime yesterday. I don't know when."

Alicia's eyebrows raised. "You don't know when you last saw your children?"

CHAPTER 4

"Where is the children's mother, Mr. Ford?" Jake asked, glancing around.

"She's not here."

"Yes, we can see that. Does she live here? Are you two married?" Jake asked.

"Well, yes and no. She did live here. But she left us a while back. I guess we are still technically married."

"I see. Have you checked to see if the kids are with her?" Jones asked.

"No. We have no contact. She left and I have no idea where she is." Nathan's eyes darted around the room, unable to make eye contact with the deputies.

"Do the kids see her?" Jones added.

"No. They don't see her." Nathan was becoming agitated. "What part of 'I have no idea where she is,' is it that you don't understand? She left about a year ago. She has not called, she has not come by to see us. No contact. Nothing. She just ran out on us."

He hadn't intended on his tone coming across the way it

had. "Hey, I'm sorry. This is just hard for me. I'm worried about my kids."

"So how do you know that she just left?" Jake asked, ignoring Nathan's previous statement.

Nathan narrowed his eyes at the deputy. "What exactly is that supposed to mean?"

"What do you think it means?" Jake replied. He kept his voice calm and deliberate. It was not his intention to agitate the man. He just wanted answers.

Ignoring the obvious attempt of the deputy to goad him, Nathan did his best to keep his cool. "I know she just left, because one day she was here, and then she wasn't."

"Did she take her items with her?" Jake asked.

"Deputy, can we talk about my children? That's why I called you here today. I'm worried about them."

Deputy Jones side eyed Jake, and responded before he had the chance to. "Of course, sir, we are here to help you find your children. So, I'm going to ask you again, when exactly was it that you last saw Ariel and Sean?"

Nathan thought about the deputy's question. "I remember that my daughter said she was going to go see her boyfriend. But I tried calling him and got no answer."

"And you haven't seen her since?" Jones asked.

"I don't think so, no."

"You don't think so?" Jake asked. He and Deputy Jones looked at each other without revealing any reaction to Nathan.

"That's what I said." Nathan clenched his teeth as he spoke.

"Sir," Jake continued, "I find it very odd that your daughter said she was going to go see her boyfriend and you don't remember if she ever came home after that. Don't you find that odd, Mr. Ford?"

Nathan gave them a one shouldered shrug. "I guess I had a bit to drink yesterday."

Jake and Alicia looked at each other again, without speaking.

Nathan noticed that time. "What?"

"Do you drink frequently, Mr. Ford?" Alicia asked him.

"Why are my drinking habits of any concern to you? I just want help finding my kids."

Ignoring his outburst, Jake continued. "What is her boyfriend's name?"

"Andrew...something."

"You don't know her boyfriend's last name?"

Jake's condescending tone was not lost on Nathan Ford, and he was getting tired of it.

"No, I don't know his last name. He's a new boyfriend and Ariel is very tight lipped about that sort of thing."

"She's thirteen. Isn't that a little young to be having a boyfriend?" Jake asked.

"So now you are criticizing my parenting? Is it against the law for a thirteen year old to have a boyfriend?"

Jake shook his head.

"Okay then, can we move on from this?"

"Do you know Andrew's phone number?" Alicia asked, lowering her voice in an attempt to calm the room.

"Yes." Nathan walked over to the kitchen table and picked up a small note, handing it to the deputy. "Here. I tried and got no answer. Maybe you'll have better luck."

"What was Ariel wearing when you saw her last?" Alicia asked him.

Nathan studied the wall behind the deputy as he tried to picture what she was wearing. "Um, jeans, I think. And her pink sweatshirt. Yes, I'm sure about the sweatshirt. Pink is her favorite color. I was the one who told her to take it, because it looked like it might rain. She argued about it, but ended up taking it."

"Okay, good." Deputy Jones wrote in her notebook. "That's helpful. It's something that might make it easier to spot her."

"Why is the hood of your car warm? Where have you been this morning? Where did you take your children, Mr. Ford?"

CHAPTER 5

"What did you do with your children?" he asked again.

Nathan's eyes met Jake's. "What? No. What are you saying?"

Nathan looked at both deputies with incredulity written all over his face.

"I've been driving all over the neighborhood looking for them." He straightened his back. "Now, if you are done with all of the accusatory questions about me, maybe you can get out there and start looking."

Nathan was holding nothing back at this point. He had enough of the attitude he was receiving from the deputies.

Alicia gave Nathan Ford a disbelieving glance. "Let me step outside to call this in." Without waiting for an answer, she walked out the front door, leaving the two men alone.

"While we are waiting for my colleague," Jake began, "why don't you show me their rooms? Maybe they left something behind that will give us a clue as to where they are."

"I've already checked their rooms. They look like they always do," Nathan told him.

Jake nodded. "You see their rooms every day. I don't. Maybe something will jump out at me. It can't hurt to try, can it?"

Jake was doing his best to keep his tone on an even keel. The man was already riled up, and worried about his children. No need to make it worse.

"Yeah, sure. Follow me."

While Jake was looking through the pink frilly bedroom that belonged to Ariel Ford, he found nothing out of the ordinary. Not even a diary of any sort.

He opened the drawers in her dresser and moved aside some of her clothing. Nothing in there that a young teen girl had hidden. He didn't know what he expected, but everything looked perfectly normal.

Ariel's jewelry box sat on top of her dresser, squarely in the middle. Jake opened it and glanced inside, picking up a few cheap looking necklaces and bracelets, before placing them back where he found them. There were several pairs of earrings in one of the compartments. In its own compartment he noticed a single silver earring. He was sure its counterpart was among the heap of other earrings in the jewelry box.

He closed it and looked through her closet while Nathan looked on. It was full of t-shirts and tank tops. Nothing looked as if it might give them a clue as to her whereabouts.

He couldn't remember ever having been in a thirteen year old girl's bedroom before. He figured it looked like it should and closed the door behind him as he exited the room.

Just as he was walking out and heading over to Sean's room next door, Alicia joined him and Nathan in the hallway.

"Let's go out into the living room to talk," Alicia directed.

The men followed her. She stopped near the front door and turned to them.

"Several more officers are on their way over. We have put out an Amber Alert for your children."

"Okay, that's good. What now?" Nathan asked.

"Now, we wait," Jones told him. She turned to Jake. "Anything in the bedrooms?"

"Nothing in Ariel's room. I didn't get to Sean's. I'll go check now." With that, he turned and headed down the hallway.

"Is there anything else you would like to tell me about the disappearance of your children?" Alicia asked Nathan.

"Like what? I don't know anything more. All I know is that I woke up and they were gone. Really, that's it. I don't think I have anything else to add."

Nathan's eyes darted toward the kitchen. The deputy noticed, but said nothing.

"Um, while we are waiting, I'm going to make something to eat, if you don't mind," Nathan told the deputy. "I haven't had much of anything since yesterday, and need to get something in my belly." He placed his left hand over his stomach and rubbed it gently.

Without waiting for a reply, he headed to the kitchen and began rummaging around in the pantry for something simple and bland to help with his lurching stomach. All he had put in it in the last twelve hours was alcohol, save for the one tiny roll he had right before calling the sheriff. He hoped something a bit more substantial would help.

Finally settling on some bread and other items, he commenced to making himself a ham and cheese sandwich, as Deputy Jones looked on. "Want one?" he asked her, holding up a slice of cheese with his bare hand.

She couldn't say no fast enough. She hadn't seen him wash his hands before making the sandwich, and watched in horror as he licked the mayonnaise off of the knife before dipping it a second time into the jar. Now her stomach lurched.

Jones couldn't take the sight of Nathan Ford's sandwich making skills a moment longer, and left the kitchen in search of Jake.

CHAPTER 6

Two more officers walked into the house. Randall, a tall black man, with closely cropped hair and muscles that his uniform could barely contain, led the way. The other man was Sheriff Manuel Garcia himself. He didn't often go out into the field, unless it was something he knew he needed to get in the middle of.

This case qualified.

"Jones, Cavanaugh," Sheriff Garcia spoke out first, "do we have any leads?"

Deputy Alicia Jones shook her head. "No sir. We've only been speaking with the father so far. Any word from those out in the field?"

"Not yet." Garcia turned to Nathan, who walked into the room eating the last of his sandwich. "Mr. Ford, I'm Sheriff Garcia. Where is your wife?"

Nathan continued chewing his last bite and swallowed it down, while the officers watched. He took his time, knowing it was irritating every last one of them, and he didn't care. Questions about his wife, when his children were missing, were getting on his last nerve.

Finally, he responded by letting out an audible huff. "Sheriff, I've already been over this with the deputies here."

"Yes, I'm sure you have. But I know something that they don't know. Something that has just come to our attention. I had almost forgotten about the case, until I heard your name, and that your children are missing."

"The case?" Nathan raised his eyebrows impossibly high. "Are you talking about my wife? Because there is no case. Nothing has changed. She ran off and I haven't heard a word from her. I didn't even know it was considered a case. Me and my kids have tried to move on with our lives. Can't you just let us do that?"

Sheriff Garcia pulled his phone from his pocket. "I have something here that I would like all of you to listen to." He pressed a green button.

"Nine-one-one. What is your emergency?"

"It's my wife. She seems to have disappeared. I can't find her anywhere."

"What is your name sir?"

"Nathan Ford. Can you help me find her?"

"How long has she been gone sir?"

"I don't know. I just woke up and she was gone."

"Have you checked with friends and neighbors? Maybe she just stepped out for a while."

"No, she didn't just step out. She's missing. She would never get up in the middle of the night and leave without tell me or the kids. I need you to find her. Something is wrong."

"Okay sir. There is a deputy on the way over."

"Oh god, what have I done?"

The call ended there. Sheriff Garcia stuck the phone back into his pocket. Nathan Ford was staring, open mouthed at the sheriff.

"Where did you get that?" Nathan asked.

"Where do you think I got it? It's from our emergency call

line. We keep all recordings indefinitely. This call sounds suspiciously similar to the call you made this morning. Now, I will ask you again, where is your wife?"

"I don't know where Cassandra is!" he yelled. "She's been gone a year. I need to focus on my kids right now."

"Maybe she and the kids are in the same place."

"What is that supposed to mean? What place?" Nathan asked. Then it dawned on him. "Oh...you don't mean...no, I'm sure they are all fine. My wife left me, that's all. Maybe she came back and took the kids in the middle of the night."

"Why now? Why would she come back after a year?" Garcia asked. "Why wouldn't she have taken the kids when she left? It seems odd that she would wait so long. Don't you think?"

"I don't know. I don't know the answers to any of your questions."

"What did you mean by 'Oh god, what have I done,' at the end of your call?" Garcia prodded.

"I...I just meant..." Nathan was having trouble figuring out how to answer that question without making things worse for himself. He knew how all of this sounded.

"What did you just mean?" Garcia prompted.

"I had been drinking that night. I was just confused, that's all. It didn't really mean anything," Nathan tried to explain.

"Do you drink a lot, Mr. Ford?" Garcia asked.

"Why do you people keep asking me that? It's none of your damn business!"

Nathan turned and walked to his kitchen. He started a pot of coffee while he attempted to calm down. He could hear the officers whispering in his living room. Once his coffee was made, he poured himself a cup and sat down at the kitchen table. He sipped at his cup while he formed a plan for finding his children. All the cops seemed to want to do was interrogate him about his wife and his drinking habits. He couldn't tell if they were actually searching for Ariel and Sean at all.

"I'll go talk to him," Deputy Jones offered. "Maybe talking to a woman will calm things down a bit. You men tend to get loud and accusatory sounding." She tilted her head and smiled. "I bet I can get him to talk."

Before the sheriff or other deputies had a chance to argue with her about it, Alicia turned on her heels and headed for the kitchen.

Deep in thought, Nathan didn't notice the deputy approaching him.

"Mind if I join you?"

Nathan jumped when she spoke. "Yes, of course. Feel free to pour yourself a cup of coffee."

"Thanks." A minute later Alicia sat down in the chair opposite Nathan's with her cup. "Mr. Ford," she began, "I apologize if we seem to not care about finding your children. Nothing could be further from the truth. In fact, we have several officers and volunteers out there right now, combing the town. The citizens of Black River know how to come together when something like this happens. Unfortunately, they've had lots of practice."

Nathan had been staring into his coffee as she spoke. His head shot up to look at her when she made the comment about them having lots of practice. "Do you think my children are dead? They caught the Black River Killer, so what are you saying?"

Jones patted the air between them. "No, of course not. I'm sure they were either taken by their mother…or ran off. We just need to figure out which."

"That's something I would like to know too," Nathan told her.

"So, why did you tell us that Cassandra left you?"

CHAPTER 7

"I told you that Cassandra left me, because that's exactly what she did." Nathan spoke through gritted teeth. It took everything in him not to yell at her. He needed her to help find his children.

"If she left you," Jones continued, "then why did you call nine-one-one? People don't normally do that when their spouse walks out."

"Yeah, I know that. I'm not an idiot. When I called, it was the middle of the night, and I had no idea where she was. I panicked, I guess. It was only later that I realized she had left me."

"And how did you come to that conclusion?"

Nathan thought for a moment before speaking. "Well, for one thing, she told one of her friends that she was unhappy in the marriage. So it seemed logical to me that she just left me."

"Does she speak with the kids? Do they have any contact with her at all?"

"No, that's the weird part. She might not have wanted to

be with me, but she loved Ariel and Sean. It is just so unlike her to never call them."

"Did she take her things with her? You know, her clothing, her makeup, that sort of thing?" Jones asked.

Nathan nodded. "Yes, she took some clothes and some makeup, I guess. Her toothbrush is gone. But most of her stuff is still here. I guess she was really pissed off at me. She didn't even stop to pack everything. She just left with a few items."

"What about money? Does she have any of her own? Has she taken any out of the bank accounts?"

Nathan took a deep breath. "I honestly don't know what she's doing about money. She was the one who always paid the bills, and probably took some money from the bank. Deputy, I've already answered all of these questions a year ago. Can we please focus on my children? Please?" He was doing his best to sound calm and be cooperative. It was not an easy task. "We can talk about Cassandra after we find my kids, okay? I promise that I'll answer everything in detail after we find Ariel and Sean."

Both Jones and Nathan turned when Deputy Jake Cavanaugh walked into the room. "Mr. Ford, isn't it true that your wife was eight months pregnant when she disappeared?"

"You know it is, Deputy. And that's the last question that I'm answering about Cassandra. If you have further questions, talk to my attorney. Now, we need to talk about my children."

Jake nodded. "Yeah, okay, we can talk about your children. How about you tell us where they really are."

Nathan slammed his fist down on the kitchen table, causing the cups of coffee to splash over. He didn't notice. "I don't know where they are!"

Nathan's sudden outburst caused the sleeves of his long

sleeved t-shirt to ride up, revealing some deep scratches on his left arm. Jake and Alicia looked at his arms and at each other with raised eyebrows.

Nathan noticed the looks on the faces of the deputies, and looked down at his own arms. He pulled his sleeves down to his hands.

"Mr. Ford, where did you get those scratches on your arm?" Jake asked him.

"I…well I…um…"

The deputies waited patiently for him to answer the question.

Nathan looked down at the coffee spilled on his table, barely noticing it. "Okay, okay, I'll tell you. But it sounds way worse than it is."

"And what is that?" Jake asked him.

"Sean lied to me about doing some chores that I told him to do. We got into an argument. I told him to go to his room and he refused. So, I grabbed him by the arm to put him in his room. He struggled to get away from me. That's when I got scratched. It's really not a big deal." Nathan couldn't look the deputies in the eyes.

"It kind of sounds like a big deal to me," Jake told him. "That sounds abusive, Mr. Ford."

Nathan looked Jake in the eyes. "Do you have children, Deputy?"

Jake shook his head. "No, I do not. What does that have to do with anything?"

"Kids can be…difficult, at times. They argue, they fight, and yes, sometimes they scratch. Ask any parent and they will agree with me. Our daughter once scratched Cassandra's eyeball with her fingernail, just goofing off at three years old. So yeah, having kids means having some injuries, here and there. You would know that if you had any children."

27

"Yeah, well I was a kid once, and don't remember injuring my parents. Ever," Jake shot back.

Nathan stared at the young man, not knowing how to answer that. He was good looking, in his twenties. He was sure that he didn't know the officer, yet somehow he knew that he had seen him before.

"You look familiar," Nathan told him. "Did you work on my wife's ca..., um her disappearance? Is that where I know you from?"

Jake shook his head. "I did not. I'm very new to this department. Now if you can please answer the..."

Jake never finished his sentence, as Nathan interrupted him, with his palm up, facing Jake. "Wait."

Nathan looked at the name tag on Jake's uniform and read it out loud. "Cavanaugh." Then it dawned on him why the deputy looked so familiar. "You wouldn't happen to be the son of Leigh Cavanaugh, would you?"

Jake averted his eyes.

Nathan Ford stood. Deputy Jones followed suit.

"Oh my god, you are. You are the son of the Black River Killer. What the hell? And you are standing here accusing me of killing my wife? What gives you the right?"

Jake moved within inches of Nathan's face.

"What my mother did, or didn't do, has no bearing on me or my job. I'm here to get answers on what happened to your wife and children. I..."

Before he could finish, Deputy Jones jumped in between the men. "Gentlemen, let's all just calm down." She turned her attention directly at Nathan. "We were talking about those scratches on your arm." She motioned to one of the other officers waiting in the living room. He walked right in. "Can you please photograph the scratches on Mr. Ford's arm here?"

The deputy nodded. He had been photographing the

house, including the children's bedrooms, and was still holding the camera.

"Where is the sheriff?" Alicia asked the officer, glancing toward the living room.

"He left. Said he had something to do." He lifted his camera. "Mr. Ford, if you wouldn't mind, can you please roll your sleeves all the way up for me?"

Alicia and Jake left the officer with Nathan Ford. They knew that he would be thorough. At the moment, they may have been suspicious of Nathan's story, but there wasn't enough to charge him with anything. Of course, that could change at any point.

CHAPTER 8

"What the hell is going on in here?"

The deputies turned toward the voice. A tall man, wearing glasses, walked in. He carried himself with some authority, as if he was always the most important person in the room.

Alicia Jones immediately noticed his full head of hair and good looks.

"Can we help you?" Jake Cavanaugh asked.

"Where is my brother?" He glanced toward the kitchen. "Never mind."

Ignoring the deputies, the man pushed past them and headed in that direction. "Nate, what is going on here? The kids are missing?"

Nathan looked up at the deputy with the camera. "Are we done here?"

"Yeah."

Nathan walked over and hugged his little brother. "Oh god, Chris, it's horrible. First Cassandra goes missing, now it's Ariel and Sean. I think I'm going to lose my mind."

Chris held his brother as he sobbed into his shoulder. He let him just cry it all out.

Finally pulling out of the embrace, Nathan wiped the tears from his face with the sleeve of his t-shirt. "What am I going to do? They think I did this."

Chris tilted his head at his big brother. "Did you?"

Chris never was one for beating around the bush. He always said what was on his mind.

Nathan's eyes widened. His voice became subdued. "How can you even ask me that? Of course not."

"Well, I find it very strange that your wife went missing last year, and now your children? I mean, what are the odds that they are completely unrelated?"

His voice louder now, "I have no idea what the odds are, but they are unrelated. At least I assume they are. Either way, I wasn't involved in any of it. I just woke up and found them gone. That's all I know, I swear."

Chris watched his brother as he spoke. "You know what, I believe you. I don't know why exactly, other than you are my big brother, but I really do believe you. With all of your issues, and there are so many, you are a good guy deep down, and the kids are lucky to have you. So now what do we do?"

Nathan let out a breath of relief. "I don't know exactly. I guess we go look for Ariel and Sean. The cops don't seem to be getting anywhere."

Digging into his pants pocket, Chris produced a set of keys. He smiled as he spun them around his index finger. "I've got the Mustang. Let's go."

Sheriff Manuel Garcia stepped in front of the men, blocking their exit. "No one is going anywhere. We can look for your children without you," he said directly to Nathan. He glanced up at Chris. "Who is your friend here?"

"Um, Sheriff, this is my brother, Chris."

"Your brother? Well, isn't that interesting?" the sheriff replied.

"What is that supposed to mean?" Chris asked. He didn't like the tone of the sheriff's words.

Ignoring Chris, Garcia turned back to Nathan. "Did you know that your wife was having an affair when she disappeared?"

Nathan nodded. "Yes, you all told me that at the time of her disappearance. It's old news. I'm over it. What I would like to know is what does that have to do with my children?"

"Well, did they also tell you who she was sleeping with?"

"No, they didn't..."

"Come on, Nathan," Chris interrupted. "Let's go. We can go talk to the kids' friends. Kids like to talk. Someone has to know something."

"No, Nathan, you need to stay here. I think you need to hear what I have to say," Garcia told them, still blocking their exit. The other deputies were starting to gather around them.

Chris, who was used to commanding a room, began to shuffle from foot to foot. Garcia noticed.

"What the hell is going on here?" Chris asked. "My niece and nephew are missing, and all you people seem to want to talk about is their mother. Aren't you even concerned about the kids?"

"Yes, of course we are concerned for the kids," Garcia replied. "We have dozens of people on the case. Black River may be a small town, but when a child goes missing, everyone comes out to help. Don't you worry about that. There won't be a stone left unturned."

"Then why do my brother and I need to stay here?" Chris asked. "We could be out there helping, instead of standing around here, getting nowhere."

"We need Mr. Ford here, to stick around, in case someone calls about the children," Garcia told him.

Chris looked the sheriff in the eyes. "You mean like a ransom call?"

Garcia nodded.

"Oh my god." Nathan ran his fingers through his graying hair. "Oh my god."

"But let's not get ahead of ourselves. I would actually like to talk to you, Nathan, about your wife's affair."

Nathan let out an audible huff. "Fine, whatever. If it will help us move past this, so we can all focus solely on Ariel and Sean, then go ahead. But I don't know anything more than I've already said."

Chris reached for his brother's arm and turned him toward the kitchen. "Come on, you don't need this. It isn't important. Let's go in the kitchen and make some phone calls."

As the two men turned their backs on the sheriff, he had more to say. "You really have no idea who your wife was sleeping with, do you, Mr. Ford?"

CHAPTER 9

The two brothers kept walking. Nathan didn't want to hear it. He didn't want to know. Cassandra's affair was old news. He had let it eat away at him for a while after she left, but he had eventually consumed enough alcohol that he put it out of his mind and decided that it didn't matter any longer. She was gone, and he doubted that she was coming back. She wouldn't even call her own children on their birthdays. That told him a lot. It told him that he didn't care about the past. In fact, if the woman walked in the door right at that moment, he would have nothing do do with her. So no, he didn't care who it was she had been sleeping with.

All he cared about was where his children were.

"Your wife was having an affair with your brother, here," Sheriff Garcia called after them.

Sheriff Garcia knew exactly what he was doing. He was starting a rift in a relationship between brothers that likely would never heal. And it didn't bother him even a little bit. It was something he knew that he needed to do to find Nathan's young children. Be damned Nathan and Chris. Their relationship was not his problem.

Nathan stopped dead in his tracks.

His heart began racing as a bead of sweat dripped down his face. He turned slowly to face his brother.

Chris' eyes were as wide as saucers. He placed his palms in the air between them, his dimples disappearing. "Now Nathan, you can't believe everything they tell you. The cops are just trying to rile you up."

Garcia stood silently, watching to see how the news would all play out between the brothers.

Nathan spoke through gritted teeth. "Are you saying it isn't true? Because that's not what I just heard."

Chris knew there was no way the cops could prove anything like that. Hell, Cassandra had been gone for a year by then. It was doubtful that she was coming back anytime soon. Probably never, by the looks of it.

"I...I don't know why you would think that. Have I ever given you any indication that I would do something like that?"

Nathan was losing patience. "You still haven't answered the question."

"No, of course I wasn't sleeping with Cassandra. There, I said it," Chris replied, widening his stance and crossing his arms.

Nathan stared into his younger brother's eyes. He watched them carefully, for any sign that he was being told something other than the complete truth. But Chris didn't flinch. Chris didn't look away. He held Nathan's gaze. The man was a rock, Nathan thought. Still...

"I don't believe you," Nathan finally announced.

Chris dropped his arms to his side. "What? Why not?"

"Because something was going on with my wife. I just didn't know what it was at the time. The cops told me she was having an affair, but that's all they told me. They never said who it was. I wasn't even sure that they knew, and I didn't ask. I think that in my mind, I just didn't want to know. Besides, once she was gone, and we were searching everywhere for her, I didn't care about any of that."

He looked at Chris, who stood silently.

"Now, I think she was messing around with you, and then you killed her to keep me from finding out."

"Whoa, wait...first you accuse me of sleeping with your wife. Now you are saying here in front of the sheriff that you think I killed her? Are you out of your damn mind?" Chris asked him. "I could never kill her. I could never kill anyone. I can't believe you even said that."

Nathan turned to Sheriff Garcia. "Why do you think my brother was sleeping with my wife? I'm not so sure now. I need something more than your say so."

"We found text messages between the two of them, that were much more intimate than what a brother and sister-in-law should be saying to each other," Garcia explained.

"I...I can explain that..." Chris began to protest.

Nathan slid his eyes toward his brother and narrowed them. "Anything else?" His question was directed at Sheriff Garcia.

"Yes. We also found nude photos of your wife that she texted to him."

"Why the hell didn't you start with that?!" Nathan yelled to the sheriff.

He then turned to his brother. "I'm going to kill you!"

CHAPTER 10

Chris put his palms in the air in a stopping motion, toward Nathan. "Whoa, just hold on now. The cops already investigated me and I was cleared."

"Maybe of murdering her. And I'm not convinced they were right about that even. But they didn't clear you of sleeping with her!" Nathan yelled.

Before any of those in attendance realized what was happening, Nathan pulled his arm back and slugged his little brother in the face with his fist. The punch landed squarely underneath Chris' left eye, causing him to lose his balance and hit the floor with a thud. He was momentarily dazed and watched stars dancing in front of his eyes. He hadn't had the chance to defend himself before being knocked to the floor.

Once Nathan pounced on him, the fight was on. Chris came back to his senses almost immediately. He didn't have a choice but to fight back. If he hadn't, Nathan might have killed him before anyone could do anything about it.

Sheriff Garcia was enjoying the show, and gave them several seconds before he intervened, holding his hand up to stop the approaching deputies. Finally, he motioned them to pull the men apart. The deputies struggled, but managed to get the men separated. They both came up flailing their arms and legs. Deputy Jones had to stifle a snicker. She thought they looked like a couple of thirteen year old girls fighting over a boy.

Once both of them were back on their feet, Sheriff Garcia spoke.

"Okay, are you two done with this nonsense now? We have two young children to find and don't have time for this."

"You are the one who started it all," Chris argued. "You had to know how this was going to turn out."

Sheriff Garcia smiled. "Yeah, I figured it wouldn't go well. But it was something I needed to do. I needed to see how you responded to the accusations. We all know about your relationship with Cassandra, and now your brother here knows as well. Did you have something to do with her disappearance also?"

"I told you I didn't," Chris replied, struggling to keep his temper in check. "What happened between us," he glanced at Nathan and dropped his gaze to his feet, "was wrong. I know that. But it wasn't murder, or anything else that you are imagining. Hell, we still don't know that she didn't just run off."

Nathan dabbed at the blood on his upper lip. Chris had given as good as he got.

"Did you two seriously have a fight? Really, at a time like this?"

They all turned to find Cassandra's sister, standing just outside their little circle.

"It's none of your business, Desiree," Nathan responded, hate spewing from his lips.

Nathan had never liked Cassandra's sister. The woman

was all of five feet tall and had short, spiked hair. She was pushy and rude, just like her hairstyle. From practically the first moment he and Cassandra began dating, Desiree was in the middle of it. In fact, she seemed to be in the middle of everything they did, during their entire relationship. The woman even dictated how the wedding would go, and how they, or Cassandra to be exact, raised their children. Desiree had an opinion about everything.

Nathan couldn't stand the sight of the woman. The only thing good to come out of his wife's disappearance, if you wanted to call it that, was that he didn't have to look at Desiree's face practically every day. She did come see Ariel and Sean occasionally, but nothing like the almost constant visits to her sister.

"Have you found my niece and nephew yet?" she asked, ignoring Nathan's comment.

"Does it look like we've found them?" Nathan made a show of looking around the room, sweeping his arm around, for dramatic effect. "Do you see them anywhere?"

"What did you do with them?" Desiree asked him. "I know how you treated those kids. And my sister. I wouldn't be surprised if you are behind the disappearance of every last one of them."

Nathan rolled his eyes toward the ceiling of the living room. "Please just go away. We don't need your help," he ordered.

It seemed as if they all already suspected him. Having Desiree show up and spout off her nonsense was just making things worse.

"Now, now," Sheriff Garcia interrupted. "I would like to hear anything that she has to say."

He looked at Desiree and smiled. She slid her eyes toward Nathan and smiled back.

"I heard Nathan arguing with his children last night, before they went missing," she told the sheriff.

A cooling breeze swept past them, coming from the open door of the house. Nathan shivered.

CHAPTER 11

All eyes shot toward Nathan. He drew in a quick breath, rubbing his left arm in an attempt at staving off the sudden chill. He was positive that every one of them noticed.

"Please, tell me more," Garcia urged Desiree.

From what Nathan could tell, the sheriff's tone seemed to border on condescending. No...he was positive that it did. The sheriff was absolutely condescending. Could Nathan blame him? Not really, no. Desiree had just dropped a bombshell on his house.

"Well, I came by last night," Desiree began. "It was around six. I came by to drop off a book Ariel had been reading at my house. I knew she would want it. I had picked her up yesterday morning and she went over to my house for a while. She does that, you know?"

Sheriff Garcia nodded. "And?" He wanted to keep the story moving.

"And, I could hear him yelling from the front yard. He was screaming actually. I walked in the front door, without knocking, and the look on Ariel's precious face was alarming. She looked scared. Terrified, really. So did Sean."

41

"Wait, I..." Nathan began.

"No, Mr. Ford, you wait." Garcia stopped him with a glare. "I want to hear the rest of her story. You can respond in a minute."

Nathan closed his mouth and stood quietly. It took every fiber in his body to do so.

"Can you tell me what they were arguing about?" Garcia asked her.

"Chores. Which is absurd when you think about it. Screaming at your children over chores. A discussion? Sure. But screaming and threatening them? It was just insane," she told them.

"He was threatening them?" Garcia prodded.

"Yeah. He told them they would be grounded for the rest of the summer and he would beat the shit out of them if they didn't get their chores done," Desiree explained.

It took everything Nathan had in him to not react to his sister-in-law's words. He drew in a deep breath, letting it out slowly. He hoped no one noticed.

"He actually said the words 'beat the shit out of' to them?" Garcia questioned.

"Wait, that wasn't serious. It was just a threat to get them to work on their chores. I swear..."

"Mr. Ford, please let her finish. If you don't, we will have to make you go outside while we listen to her story."

"This is my house!" Nathan yelled.

Garcia didn't seem the slightest bit interested in hearing Nathan's side of things. "I'm warning you."

Nathan shook his head and averted his eyes. He looked over at his brother, Chris, who was staring at him. The look was unnerving to Nathan. It was as if Chris was convicting him of murdering his children right then and there.

All this time, Deputies Alicia Jones and Jake Cavanaugh were standing behind Nathan and Chris, watching and listening to everything. They were ready to pounce if another altercation started between the brothers.

Sheriff Garcia turned back to Desiree. "What did you do when you heard this argument?"

"I told Nathan to stop screaming at his children. I also told him that I wanted to take Ariel and Sean to my house for the night."

"And did you?" Deputy Jake jumped in.

"No, obviously not. Otherwise we would all be having an entirely different conversation. Or, more likely, no conversation at all. Don't you think?" Desiree directed her sarcasm to Jake.

Her snarky tone was not appreciated by the deputy, and he was about to tell her so. Deputy Jones could sense what was about to take place, and patted him on the shoulder. He tensed for just a moment, then his shoulders relaxed. Without saying anything, Jake knew what she was trying to convey. And she was right, he needed to take a breath and think about his next steps. Having half a dozen or so witnesses to his almost outburst, was a bad idea. A really bad idea. Even more so since it was his first day on the job.

Sheriff Garcia intercepted. "Okay, so if you were obviously concerned about your niece and nephew, why didn't you take them to your house?" he asked her.

She looked over at Nathan, and could see the pain on his face. She didn't care. He was a monster, as far as she was concerned. She knew, with every fiber of her being, that he had killed her sister. She and Cassandra were very close. She couldn't fathom a world where Cassandra would just run off, leave her children, and never contact her sister again. No, it was something she knew that Cassandra would never do. There was only one explanation for her disappearance: Nathan.

"I didn't take them to my house because Nathan wouldn't

let me. He told me that they were just having a normal father, daughter argument, and that it was none of my business. She was a teenager after all. At least that's what he said to me," Desiree told them all.

Everyone turned to Nathan for his side of the events.

Sheriff Garcia spoke first. "Tell us what happened last night."

How in the world was he going to smooth this one over, Nathan wondered. His wife was missing. His children were missing. It looked bad. He knew it. He was no fool. And with the accusation that he had been fighting with the kids right before they both disappeared, he could be done for.

Nathan scrambled for the right words.

"Mr. Ford, did you hear me? Can you explain what happened last night?" Sheriff Garcia prodded.

"Yeah yeah, okay, I will. Just give me a second, will ya?" Nathan turned and paced to the far end of the room. When he turned back the way he had come, every eye in the room was watching him intently. He could tell immediately that anything he had to say would be met with disbelief. But he had to try.

Deputy Jones got a call and stepped outside to take it. Not a full minute later, she stuck her head inside the house and motioned for Jake and the sheriff to join her outside.

"One moment," the sheriff told Nathan, holding up his index finger. "We will be right back. Don't go anywhere."

"You are all in my house. Where am I going to go?" Nathan instantly regretted his words. The last thing he needed was to come off as argumentative to the sheriff.

Garcia ignored the man, and joined Alicia and Jake on the front steps.

"They found the boy," Deputy Jones told her colleagues.

CHAPTER 12

"They found Sean?...Oh no," Jake Cavanaugh responded. "I'm not going to like where this is headed, am I?"

Deputy Jones shook her head. "No, you definitely are not."

Jake hung his head low.

"Well, come on. Let's go inside and give them the news," Sheriff Garcia told them.

The men followed Alicia into the house. They walked up to the group, which consisted of Nathan, Chris, and Desiree, as well as a couple of deputies. The living room was starting to feel quite cramped.

Deputy Jones interrupted the murmur of the group. "Excuse me, Mr. Ford, can we have a word with you please?" She gestured toward the open front door with a flick of her head. "Outside."

"Um, yeah, I guess."

As Nathan made his way through the group and toward the front door, he could feel a lead weight in his stomach. It wasn't going to be good news. Pulling him to the side, away from everyone else, was going to be his worst nightmare. He took a deep breath as he exited the house.

Closing the door behind him, Jake joined Alicia and Nathan Ford in the front yard.

"Okay, what is this about? Did you find my children?" He braced for the worst.

"I'm afraid that I have bad news. We found Sean's body," Alicia Jones told him as stoically as she could muster.

"Oh my god. No, this can't be happening."

Nathan's legs gave way and he fell to his knees in the soft grass. He covered his face in his hands and began to sob.

The two deputies just stood there, not really knowing what to do. Really, there was nothing they could do. He just needed some time to let it all out.

The people inside the house all heard the commotion on the front lawn, and spilled out, one by one.

"What is going on out here?" Desiree asked. "Did you find the kids? Please god, tell me they are all right." She glanced over at Nathan, still on his knees, and took in a quick breath.

Jake pulled Desiree and Chris to the side, and kept his voice low. "We found Sean. I'm sorry to say that he's dead."

"What? No, that can't be right," Desiree exclaimed. "Please, tell me that isn't true!"

Though Chris had never been a fan of Desiree, he wrapped his arms around her as they both cried for a nephew they would never see again. Sean had been a smart, funny kid, that they all loved being around. There was never a dull moment when Sean was in the house.

After releasing Desiree, Chris walked over to his big brother, who had stood back up by the time he got there. Yeah, they had just had a fistfight minutes prior, but he didn't care. His brother was in pain, and he was going to be there for him. The brothers embraced. And cried.

"Oh god, Chris, what am I going to do without my little boy?"

Chris pulled out of the embrace and wiped his brother's tears with his hand. "I don't know. I just don't know. How can this be happening?"

Nathan looked over at Deputy Jones. "Can you tell me what happened to Sean? Anything at all?"

"Mr. Ford, would you like to walk over there," she pointed to an area on the other side of the yard, "and talk privately?"

Nathan looked at his brother, and at Desiree, who had made her way over to them, and at the others. "No. Thank you, but it's not necessary. We all love Sean, and everyone here is going to know anyway. You might as well tell us all together."

The look on Nathan's face was of pure agony. It was at that moment that Alicia Jones very much doubted that he had killed his own son. And if she was wrong, then Nathan Ford deserved an Oscar.

So, she wondered, if she was right, then who killed him? It was an almost unheard of occurrence for two children to be taken at the same time. That would take some planning, and possibly, no...probably, two or more people to pull it off.

Deputy Jones needed to answer Nathan's question about the death of his son in the most gentle, caring way she knew how. She had no children, and couldn't even fathom what he was going through, but she knew it had to be a horrible experience for him. It would be for any parent.

"His bod...um Sean, will still need to be examined, and have an autopsy done, but the preliminary examination seems to indicate that he was...strangled. I'm very sorry for your loss," she added quickly.

"Noooo!" It was Desiree who responded in the most outspoken way. She knew he was dead, but hearing the manner in which her beloved nephew died, was almost too much for her to bear. It was an image that would float around in her head until her own dying day.

In a surprising move, it was Nathan who comforted his sister-in-law this time. He put his arm around her shoulders and she tilted her head to rest on his shoulder. He squeezed her arm. Sure, he and Desiree weren't friends, but they were family, and he knew she was hurting every bit as much as he was.

It wasn't the first time that Deputy Jones had to give a distraught family member bad news, and it certainly wouldn't be the last. She dreaded it each and every time. Most officers she knew hated the task more than anything. They would rather have gang members shooting at them, than to have to face a grieving parent.

"Who would do that?" Nathan asked, barely above a whisper. "Who would want to hurt my little boy? Sean never did anything to anyone. What kind of monster could do this?"

CHAPTER 13

Responding to Nathan Ford's question about his son, Deputy Alicia Jones spoke up first. "We don't know who the culprit is just yet. But I promise you that we will do our best to find him. You can count on that."

"What about my daughter? What about Ariel? You didn't mention her. Was she found also?" Nathan prayed that the answer was no. As long as she wasn't found, she could still be alive, out there somewhere in the world.

Alicia shook her head. "No, we haven't found her yet. But we are working on it. We hope to have some news about her very soon. We won't stop looking until we find her. That is a promise from me."

Alicia knew that she should never make such promises to a family member of a crime victim, especially to a terrified parent. But she couldn't help herself. Besides, she knew that it was the truth. She would never stop looking for Ariel. Not ever.

"I'm very sorry for your loss also," Sheriff Manuel Garcia told Nathan and his family. "We will do everything we can to find her. Excuse me now."

Garcia stepped away from the family. "Okay, everyone!" Sheriff Garcia shouted to his deputies. "All of you gather 'round." Almost everyone was standing with the group. Garcia moved to a corner of the yard to speak with the deputies out of earshot of the family. They all followed.

"All of you, hurry up." Garcia motioned them over, using his hands in a 'move your ass' sort of way. "Okay, listen." He kept his voice low. "We have to do whatever we can to find this young girl, before she succumbs to the same fate as her brother. I don't care what you do, but get out there in the forest and leave no pine cone unturned. Look behind every rock, tree, hill, muskrat, whatever. We cannot leave the forest and come back here to tell that grieving father that we couldn't find her."

A couple of the deputies turned toward the family at that point. Nathan, Chris, and Desiree were all watching them with interest.

"Does anyone have any questions?" Garcia asked.

A chorus of 'no sirs' rang out.

"Great. Then get out there and find Ariel Ford."

The deputies dispersed toward their waiting cars.

Very early the next morning, before the sun had even begun to peek over the horizon, the skies were still a dark gray and there was a distinct chill in the air.

Deputy Jones stood with her hot coffee in hand, in the parking lot next to the forest. She peered into the thickness of the trees, but couldn't see much. Dark trees and shadows for the most part were the only things in front of her. She couldn't see them, but she could hear the searchers making their way through the darkness. The crunching under their feet told her that everyone was on the move.

Alicia lifted her head, listening to the searchers calling for Ariel. Off in the distance, her name seemed to be wafting on the breeze.

Though it was not even 5 a.m., there were dozens of deputies searching the woods. Many came from surrounding towns to help. For some, it was even their day off, which didn't matter one bit. They wanted to be there to help find the missing 13 year old girl for the grieving father. The man who had already lost his young son. None of them could bear to see a father lose both of his children within days of each other.

His missing wife was an entirely different matter altogether. Some believed Nathan Ford was responsible for Cassandra's disappearance, while others believed he was just the recipient of bad luck. Extremely bad luck.

Still…Sheriff Manuel Garcia found the probability of three out of four people in one family to go missing, at two different times, about a year apart, to be highly suspicious. He was keeping a close watch on one Nathan Ford.

In addition, there were more than 100 civilian volunteers roaming the forest. Everyone wanted to help bring the girl home. Moms, dads, grandparents, and even young children were among those who had climbed out of bed at 4 a.m. to join the search. Alicia couldn't help but be moved by the generosity of those living in Black River.

Every one of them had lived through the era of the Black River Killer. Many wondered if there was a copycat, since the killer had been apprehended and now spent her days in maximum security. She would never be free to wander the forests of Black River again.

After that reign of terror, the townspeople couldn't help but want to get involved in finding Ariel Ford. It was the only thing they could do really.

The day was dismal for searching the forest. It was windy

and the rain came down in a drizzle, seemingly from every-where. Every thing and every one was absolutely soaked to the bone. And freezing. There was no way to avoid it. The ominous looking dark clouds above told a story of impending weather to come that was going to make the current conditions seem like a warm, sunny day at the beach.

All in all, the officers on site were eternally grateful that any volunteers showed up at all. It could be worse. They could be searching the soggy woods all on their own. And that could last so many more hours. So yes, the volunteers seemed like a blessing to them.

CHAPTER 14

Deputy Alicia Jones headed up the search. She had a command post set up in the parking lot at the entrance to the forest hiking trails and campgrounds. Everyone reported to her and Jake Cavanaugh.

The two of them had spent over two hours setting up tables, chairs, and an actual tent to work in. There was no way that they would be able to get anything done in the rain and wind. The only thing missing was a couple of space heaters to make the place more toasty. Oh well, she had suffered through worse, a lot worse, to get the job done.

"You know, this place feels like those army camps you see on TV," Jake told her, surveying their handiwork from inside the tent. "You know, the ones you see set up overseas in the middle of the desert somewhere," he explained. "I fully expect to get orders over the radio to send out the troops to go after the enemy."

Alicia Jones smiled. "Well, that's pretty much what we are doing, don't you think? We are sending out the troops, aka officers and volunteers, to find Ariel, so we can figure out who Sean's killer is."

"You have a point there," Jake told her with a nod.

"Excuse me." Desiree plopped four boxes, all stacked on top of each other, onto the table in front of the deputies. "I brought donuts for everyone. I hope you don't mind."

"Of course not. This is great," Alicia told her, grabbing the boxes and spreading them out on the table next to her. "These won't last long," she added.

Desiree smiled. "Oh this isn't all. I have a dozen more boxes in the back of my SUV." She looked up at Jake. "Would you mind helping me?"

Desiree didn't wait for a response and exited the tent. Jake smiled at Alicia and followed dutifully. Ten minutes later, all of the donuts were inside the tent. They had the original four boxes spread out, and open, and the rest of the boxes stacked up in the corner. It fell on Jake to be in charge of replacing the boxes as they were emptied.

Not two minutes later, six of the volunteers made quick work of emptying the first box of donuts. They definitely wouldn't last long.

After four hours searching the damp woods, nothing had turned up and morale was waning. A few of the volunteer searchers had given up, grabbed a couple of donuts, and skulked their way home in order to thaw out in front of their fireplaces.

"Deputy, Deputy!" came a shout from somewhere deep in the forest. The voice sounded young, like a teenage girl. "I think I found something!"

"Deputy! Come over here!" the girl yelled. "There's something in the bushes!"

Randall, the tall deputy with large muscles picked his way through the mud over to where the girl was standing. His large frame and sized 16 boots, caused the mud to latch onto his feet like wet concrete. It was a struggle to get through it, as the mud sucked at his boots with each step. After several minutes, he made his way to her.

She was looking down at something behind some bushes. He stood next to her and followed her pointing finger to the spot on the ground.

"There. Do you see it?" she asked, with a shaky voice. Her eyes were wide, and her face was pale. The girl wrapped her arms around her mid-section and held on tightly. The deputy couldn't quite tell if she was cold from the weather or steeling herself for what laid below.

By the look on her face, Randall fully expected to find the body of Ariel Ford lying behind the bush. But that wasn't what he saw.

"What is that, Deputy? A jacket, maybe?" the girl asked. "I didn't touch it, like you told us not to."

He nodded and looked down at the girl, who was at least a foot shorter than he was. "Yeah, that could be it."

Not wanting to get any of the searchers excited about what was found, he told the girl to just stand there and not say anything to anyone. Randall pulled a pair of latex gloves from his coat pocket. He donned the gloves and knelt down to get a better look.

Making a concerted effort to not disturb anything around it, he reached down and just barely touched it. "It's a sweat-shirt, actually," he told the girl. Though he wasn't entirely sure why he felt it necessary to give her any details.

Looking back up at her, he noticed the crowd gathering. He realized then that warning her again to keep quiet was probably unnecessary. Several people had heard her yelling to him when she spotted the sweatshirt. There was no way that he would be able to contain everyone who was beginning to surround them.

"Go get one of the deputies in the tent," he ordered the same teen girl.

She smiled and tore off in a sprint. Despite the circumstances they had found themselves in, that made him smile. The girl was obviously thrilled to be part of the investigation.

Standing back up, Randall used the palms of his hands to convey to the small crowd to back up. "Guys, we need to be careful here. This might be evidence and I can't have any of you stomping all over the scene."

The crowd backed up. Randall stood guard over the sweatshirt. In the rain. In the cold. He wasn't about to screw this up.

As they all stood there waiting for someone with evidence bags, Randall had to field questions from the crowd.

"Is that Ariel Ford's sweatshirt?"

"Is Ariel dead?"

"Have you found Ariel?"

"Did her father kill her?"

Randall answered every single question the same way. "I cannot comment on an ongoing investigation."

It didn't matter though. The questions kept coming. He let out a breath of relief when he saw Deputy Alicia Jones arrive.

CHAPTER 15

"What do we have here?" she asked Randall, standing next to him and looking down at the item in the mud.

He leaned in and whispered. "It's a pink sweatshirt. You know, just like the one she was wearing when she disappeared."

Jones scanned the crowd. She understood why he whispered, and she felt the need to do something about all the looky-loos. "Hey guys, we just have something to bag up for evidence here. We don't know anything further. Please continue searching for the girl."

Not a single person took a step.

"Hey! I wasn't kidding. Move it along. We have work to do here!" Deputy Jones didn't have time for nonsense. It was cold and rainy, and she just wanted to get the sweatshirt bagged and get the hell out of the weather. Her own sweatshirt was soaked and heavy. She moved quickly.

That did it. Amongst a chorus of "okays" and other grumblings from the crowd, they slowly dispersed.

"Did they give you any trouble?" she asked Randall.

He shrugged. "Not really. They asked a few questions

about the girl, but I told them that I could not answer any questions about an ongoing investigation. They didn't like it, but that's all they got out of me."

She nodded. "Good job."

After photographing the pink sweatshirt and surrounding area, Alicia handed an evidence bag to Randall and he commenced collecting it for inspection. Maybe there was some evidence on it that would lead them to Ariel.

"You know," Randall began, as he worked at collecting the sweatshirt, "I find it very odd that her sweatshirt would be lying here in the middle of the forest. In weather like this, why would she take it off?"

"Maybe it wasn't up to her," Alicia replied back, watching Randall's work. He was an excellent deputy, but she was standing there anyway. It never hurt to have another set of eyes on something that could be really important to their investigation.

Two days later, the results of Sean Ford's autopsy came back.

"Dammit!" Sheriff Manuel Garcia exclaimed after reading the autopsy report. "I was really hoping that we were wrong about Nathan Ford. Come on Jones, Cavanaugh. We have a father to talk to."

As the trio headed out of the sheriff's station, Cassandra Ford's sister, Desiree was just walking up the steps toward the front door. The rain had moved on and the day was hot and sunny. She wore a wide brimmed hat and dark sunglasses. Her yellow sundress perfectly complemented the ensemble.

"Excuse me, Sheriff? Can I talk to you for a minute?" she asked, as they passed her on the steps. None of them seemed to have noticed her.

All three stopped and turned toward her. They certainly did have a lot on their minds, but to completely not notice the sister-in-law of a prime suspect, was unlike them.

"Yes, of course," the sheriff replied. "Desiree, right?"

She nodded. "Yes, right. I wanted to tell you about something that my sister once told me. It's been a while, and I had almost forgotten about it, but I thought that you should know."

"Is it important in the investigation of this case?" he asked her.

"Yes, I think it is."

The knock on the front door didn't even register to Nathan Ford. He was sitting in the large, comfortable lounge chair in his living room. He didn't care that it was a purple and orange eyesore. It was quite comfortable and his favorite place to sit. The television was on, but he wasn't watching it. In fact, if someone asked him at that moment what was showing, he would have had no clue. His mind was elsewhere.

He had been lost in thought. When he and Cassandra met, during college, she was so beautiful. He remembered her long blonde, stick straight hair, and blue eyes. He sat behind her in their economics class and he had a crush on her from the moment she walked in and took the seat in front of him. She turned, and with a smile, had asked him for a pen, explaining that she had forgotten to grab one.

Nathan had three of them in his backpack and enthusiastically gave her the one he had been using.

It was all over for him at that point. He was over the moon, hopelessly in love.

Not long after that, the two of them began dating. She

was friendly, outgoing, and the life of any gathering the two of them attended. He had no idea what she saw in him, but he was damn glad that she found something worthwhile. They married in a small ceremony right after college. And not long after that, welcomed baby Ariel into the world.

It had been the best time of his life.

And now, the worst time of his life was underway.

The incessant pounding on the front door finally startled Nathan back to reality.

He shuffled, barefoot, to the front door. His eyes widened at the sight of the sheriff, and two of his deputies on the front porch. All three had stern looks, and that terrified him.

"Is there news about Ariel?" he asked, before anyone had a chance to say anything. He held his breath.

"No." Garcia spoke first. "This is about Sean. His autopsy results are in."

Nathan's face went stark white. By the faces of the officers in front of him, it wasn't going to be good news for Nathan. Not that any autopsy results on his son would be good news, but it was worse than he could expect. He just knew it.

"Can we come in?" Garcia asked.

Nathan opened the door wider and moved to the side, as the trio walked in. His knees were unsteady. Nathan made a concerted effort to stand straight and tall. He would not let this get him down. He had lost Sean, which was a horrible nightmare, and there was absolutely nothing he could do about that. But he still had Ariel, and needed to be strong for her.

Upon reaching the living room, they all turned toward him, while Nathan closed the front door.

Nathan studied the faces of the three officers standing in front of him. They were hard to read. Not one of them betrayed what they were thinking.

"So…what is it that I need to know about the autopsy that brought three people here to tell me?"

Sheriff Garcia looked over at Deputy Jones and gave her a slight nod.

Jones spoke up. "We found skin underneath Sean's fingernails."

CHAPTER 16

"Okay." Nathan stood staring at them. "So what does that mean exactly?"

"It means," Sheriff Garcia piped in this time, "that we need to take another look at the wounds on your arms."

Without thinking, Nathan's eyes darted to his bare arms. He was wearing only a t-shirt and shorts. His arms revealed several healing scratches. The three officers followed suit and all stared at his arms.

He dropped his arms to his sides and turned them so that the scratches weren't visible to the officers standing in front of him. "I already told you about my disagreement with Sean, and that he scratched me. You remember that, right?"

He looked into the eyes of each person standing in front of him. One by one they averted their gaze to the floor in front of him.

"Someone speak." Nathan's voice was rising. "I know you remember. It was just a disagreement between me and my son. Nothing more. He got squirrelly on me and that's how I got scratched. Please, you have to believe me. I would never, not in a million years, ever hurt my son. I love him." As much as he tried to keep his voice on an even keel, the desperation in Nathan's voice was evident.

By this time, tears were threatening to spill down Nathan's face.

"We are still waiting for the tests on the skin under his fingernails to come back," Sheriff Garcia told him. "But by the looks of those arms of yours, I feel fairly certain there is going to be a match to you."

Nathan nodded. "Yes, it's going to match me. That's what I've been trying to tell you!" He could no longer contain his frustration. "Are any of you even listening to me?"

"Yes, Mr. Ford, we heard you," Garcia responded. "But you have to understand our side of this. We have seen this sort of thing before, and know very well that your story of a disagreement where your son scratched you, could just be your cover story. This certainly wouldn't be the first time a fight between a parent and child got out of hand. And it wouldn't be the first time someone lied to us."

The three officers studied Nathan for a reaction.

He took a deep breath and let it out slowly before responding. "There was no fight. I'm not lying. Sean is nine years old...was nine years old," he corrected.

Nathan turned his head away after saying that, in order to not show any weakness in front of the officers. He was worried that they would mistake his words for some sort of confession. That was the last thing he needed. Quickly gathering his composure, he turned back to look at them. They were still watching him, curiosity in their eyes.

"You want to tell us again what happened?" Jake Cavanaugh asked.

Nathan spoke slowly. "As I have already explained to you all, repeatedly at this point, I told Sean to vacuum the floor. When I asked him later about it, he lied to me. It was quite obvious that he hadn't touched the floor."

The gaze of all three officers instinctively dropped to scan the floor. It definitely had not been vacuumed recently. But then again, the debris could have been caused by the dozen or so people who had trampled through the house over the last couple of days.

Because of that, there was no way to tell if the kid had actually lied to his father and caused a fight between the two.

Nathan saw their reaction. "I know the floor is filthy. I've had other things on my mind lately."

Jones nodded. "Of course."

"Such as, when are you going to find my daughter? Instead, you are here wasting my time, and your time, going over an incident that has nothing to do with nothing. Sean is gone. As much as I want that to change, I know that it never will. I need to focus on Ariel. She's my main concern now. What are you doing to find her?"

Nathan looked into each face standing in front of him.

"We would like to know what *you* are doing to find your daughter," Jake asked, looking at Nathan from head to toe and taking in the t-shirt and shorts. Glancing over at the television only a few feet away, Jake continued. "Seems to us that you are doing absolutely nothing. From what I can see, you are not a bit concerned about finding your daughter. Is that because you know she is already dead?"

"How dare you say that to me! I have no idea where my daughter is and I haven't had a wink of sleep in days. If you remember correctly, you told me not to leave the house, in case the kids come back, or there is a ransom call or some-thing. I do nothing but worry about her. And even though you told me not to, I've been out every single day searching the streets for her. I have talked to every one of her friends, including their parents. I've even passed out fliers all over town."

Nathan looked at each officer, one by one. "You've seen the fliers, haven't you?"

They all nodded.

"Who the hell do you think did that? It wasn't you all, that's for sure. So don't you dare stand there and tell me that I don't care about my daughter, and that I'm doing nothing to find her." That last remark was aimed squarely at Jake Cavanaugh.

"What I'd like to know is what exactly you all are doing to find Ariel?" Nathan added.

"Okay, okay." Sheriff Garcia attempted to diffuse the situation by patting the air down in front of him. "Let's all just calm down here. We need to focus on the task at hand. We are doing everything we can to find your daughter." He turned to Deputy Jones and gave her the 'go ahead' nod.

CHAPTER 17

"Mr. Ford," Jones replied to him, "you can be assured that we are doing everything we can to find your daughter. There are dozens of people out there actively looking for her as we speak, as well as hundreds of volunteers. You don't need to worry about that. We won't give up until she is found." She gave him a reassuring smile. "Now, please continue with your story about the scratches on your arm."

Nathan looked down at his arms once again. "Yeah, okay fine. Where was I?"

"You said Sean hadn't vacuumed, like you told him to," Jones prompted.

"Oh yeah. Um, so we started to argue about it. We were getting nowhere, which was why I finally told him to go to his room, and he wouldn't. He just stayed on the couch and crossed his arms, all defiant like. So I...I..." Oh boy, Nathan knew how the next part was going to sound. But he knew he needed to tell them everything. If he left anything out, and they found out later, it wouldn't look good for him.

"You what?" Garcia asked, trying to move the story along.

"I…I took his arm to get him up off the couch."

"Took his arm…or grabbed his arm?" Garcia asked. "Because last time you used the word 'grabbed' when describing the encounter."

"I did?" Nathan tried to remember their conversation from before. He couldn't recall the exact word he used. "Well, either way, I did take his arm to get him up. That's when he started to fight me. You know, struggling to get away. And he was yelling at me. I mean, the kid was a bit out of control. He scratched me as I tried to hang onto him. Once I got a good grip, I escorted him to his room. That's it. End of story."

For a moment, Nathan seemed satisfied with his retelling of the events that had taken place. But as he stood there and watched the reactions of the officers, he suddenly wasn't so sure that he didn't just stick both feet into his big fat mouth.

"It's really not a big deal," Nathan added.

"Not a big deal?" Sheriff Garcia repeated. "Your son is dead, Mr. Ford. And that's not a big deal?"

Nathan's face heated up. "No. Of course the death of my son is a big deal. I would never say otherwise. I love my son more than anything, and I am devastated here. My life will never be the same. And my daughter's life will never be the same…if you find her and bring her back to me," he tried to explain. "I just meant that the disagreement Sean and I had was no big deal in the scheme of things. It was just the typical dad and kid fight…um…disagreement. It happens. Really, officers, that's all I meant."

Garcia, Jones, and Cavanaugh kept silent.

"Can you please turn your attention on someone else? I did not harm my son in any way. I would never do that."

Jake Cavanaugh jumped in. "Why is it that every time we ask you a question, you deflect onto someone else? You have someone in particular in mind?"

Nathan gritted his teeth. "No I don't have anyone in particular in mind. Don't you think I would have told you if I did? I'm telling you to look into someone else because I didn't do it!"

He took a calming breath before continuing. "Now, can we please focus on my daughter? We might still have a chance to bring her home alive."

Not missing a beat, Jake continued. "Where is your daughter, Mr. Ford?" He never broke eye contact with the father.

"I don't know! How many times do I have to tell you people that?"

"When was the last time you saw her?" Jake continued.

"Like I said before, she went to see her boyfriend. Why do you keep asking me the same questions over and over? My answers aren't going to change."

Sheriff Garcia turned to the deputies. "Jones, come with me. Cavanaugh, stay here. Keep your eyes on this one." Garcia pointed directly at Nathan.

Without waiting for a reply, Sheriff Garcia headed for the front door. He didn't feel the need to turn around. He knew that Alicia would follow him out. No questions asked.

Once the pair reached the front yard, he stopped and faced her. "I want you to find that boyfriend. I know you have called him, and even stopped by his house, without any luck. But I'm tired of being jerked around. Get over there and find him. His whole family didn't suddenly go poof in the night."

Garcia's hands flew up in front of him, facing Alicia, making a dramatic gesture while opening all ten fingers. Sort of like what a magician would do. Poof.

"Sir, I have been trying to locate him," Alicia tried to explain.

"Do I look like I care? Talk to everyone in town who

knows them and find out where they went. Don't come back until you do."

She nodded. "Yes sir."

Without another word, Alicia Jones jumped in her car and headed toward the boy's house. No need to look at her notes. She knew exactly where he lived.

Finding Jake Cavanaugh and Nathan Ford still in the exact spots that the sheriff had left them in, he smiled to himself. It made him happy when people did exactly what he told them to do.

"Cavanaugh, come here."

Once they were across the room, he continued. "Go talk to people who knew the girl. Teachers, neighbors, parents of her friends, everyone. I don't care who they are, if they ever met her, then talk to them. I want to know more about her. Who was she? What were her hobbies? Did she hang out with boys? Is she sleeping around? Did she smoke or drink? That sort of thing."

"Um, sir, she is only thirteen," Jake told him.

"Yes, I know. I also had sisters who were thirteen once. So I know how they can be. Now go do what I said."

Jake headed out the door.

Three hours later, he had spoken with more than a dozen people. Everyone thought she was an angel. Her teachers couldn't say enough nice things about her. The parents of her friends said they felt safe with Ariel around their daughters.

He even spoke directly with her friends. They all said the same thing. She was not quite the angelic child that all the adults thought she was. She did drink occasionally, didn't smoke as far as they knew. She liked the boys, but they were not aware of her actually sleeping with any of them.

So there it was. She showed one personality with her friends, and an entirely different one to the adults in her life.

But isn't that what all teenagers do?

Jake wasn't convinced that there were any red flags. She just seemed like the typical teen to him.

CHAPTER 18

Andrew's neighborhood consisted of row after row of nondescript tract housing. With no more than four different home designs, the overall ambience of the area was a slow, almost sluggish feeling. Each house was in a varying shade of beige.

Each lawn was perfectly manicured, with tall oleander bushes separating many of the houses. A stick straight side-walk lined the street. Not a crack or weed to be found.

Three young girls with multi-colored helmets rode their bicycles up and down the street, turning their bikes into a perfect circle every now and again, before continuing up the road.

Two boys, no more than twelve, stood in the middle of the street tossing a football back and forth to each other, paying no mind to the traffic. Not that there was any, really. Sometimes it would be hours before a car passed by. Even then, the boys were annoyed that they had to stop for a few precious seconds before resuming.

Deputy Jones saw the boys the moment she turned onto the street. They didn't notice her until she got close to them and gave them just the slightest of warning from the siren in her car. It was just enough to get their attention.

It stunned her that they hadn't noticed her at all. Especially since one of the boys was facing right toward her while throwing the ball to his friend. After the warning, the boys looked at her, took in the sheriff's patrol car, and seemingly unconcerned that a deputy was glaring at them, moved to the sidewalk so she could pass. Alicia waved at them as she went by. They returned the favor.

Parking in front of Andrew's nondescript beige house with white trim, the very house she had been to at least three separate times over the past few days, the deputy spotted a silver SUV in the driveway. The back was wide open, as well as the two passenger side doors.

This was her chance. She had finally caught them at home. But she waited to see what the family was up to before going inside. She knew that time was of the essence in finding Ariel Ford, but she also needed to be smart about the whole thing. Just pouncing on them might prove to be a mistake. If Andrew was involved in her disappearance in any way whatsoever, and if his parents knew that, they might get spooked.

Her patrol car was parked mostly in front of the house next door, partially obscured by the oleander bushes that separated the two houses.

She watched as a woman walked out of the house, dressed in a powder blue t-shirt, tan capris, and white sandals.

Two girls, who appeared to be about 10 and 12 years old, roughly, followed the woman out to the car. A moment later, a teenage boy joined them, grabbed a suitcase and wheeled it inside. Alicia figured that had to be just who she was looking for.

As she watched, nothing unusual took place. It appeared they were just a family unpacking after a trip. That could explain whey they had been nowhere to be found over the past several days.

The question was, had they been on an innocent family vacation, or had they been on the run? The latter seemed unlikely, since they came back so quickly. A guilty complex maybe?

One thing Alicia did notice was that she hadn't seen a man anywhere. Was there even one around? Still sitting in her patrol car, she flipped through her notebook. Nothing. No information on a boyfriend of the mother at all. That didn't really mean anything as she hadn't taken the time to investigate the family. She only wanted to ask Andrew if he knew anything about Ariel's whereabouts. For all Alicia knew, Ariel had been on the trip with the family.

Ariel's father certainly didn't know if she had gone off on a vacation with them.

But the girl was nowhere in sight. It was time she found out if anyone knew anything about Ariel Ford, and where she might be.

Deputy Jones climbed out of the patrol car and approached the family. The mother was leaning into the car, gathering trash into a bag. She hadn't noticed anyone approaching.

The youngest of the girls spotted her first.

"Um, Mom," she said while pulling at the hem of her mother's t-shirt, "there's a police person here."

"What?" the woman called with her head still sticking inside the back seat.

"She said that there is a police officer here," Deputy Jones responded, in the most authoritative voice she could muster.

That got the mother's attention. She backed out of the car and stood up, turning to face the stranger in uniform standing before her.

"Um hi, officer. Sorry, I didn't see you there. What can I help you with?"

Alicia nodded. "I'm Deputy Jones. I'm here about the disappearance of Ariel Ford."

The woman's eyes widened. "The what? Ariel is missing?"

"Yes. And her brother, Sean, was found de..." Her words trailed off when she noticed the wide eyed look on the little girl's face. "Um, can we talk alone?" Alicia never removed her gaze from the little girl.

The mother glanced down at her daughter. "Yeah, of course. Honey, go in the house. I'll be in when I'm done here."

The girl took one more look at the deputy and did as her mother ordered.

Both women stood in silence until Sandy was safely in the house, and out of earshot.

CHAPTER 19

"Okay now, deputy, what is this all about? Is Ariel really missing? And what were you going to say about her little brother?" the woman asked.

"Can I get your name please?" Alicia asked her.

She needed to just double check that she had the right person. It wouldn't be the first time she had gotten that wrong. Alicia once spent several minutes questioning the brother of a suspect, instead of the suspect himself, before she realized her mistake. Sheriff Garcia chewed her out for that one. She couldn't blame him. It was a stupid mistake. She knew it, and vowed to never let it happen again.

"Yeah sure. It's Cathi Mosley. Now please, tell me what's going on?"

Alicia Jones had already done some background work on the Mosley family. She knew that Cathi's husband had died years ago in a car accident. What she didn't know was whether Cathi was dating anyone. It could be important.

"Does anyone else live here, besides you and your three children?"

Cathi tilted her head as she contemplated the question. "What does that have to do with anything?"

"Just answer the question, Mrs. Mosley," Alicia ordered.

Cathi waved her hand in the air dismissively. "Okay, fine. No one lives here besides me and my children. My husband died a few years ago, you know. Now, why aren't you telling me anything?"

"Like I said, Ariel Ford is missing. She's been gone for four days now. Do you know anything about that?"

"Me? No. Why would I know anything about that?" Cathi's voice was a mixture of fear and annoyance.

"Because your son is seeing her."

Cathi shook her head. "Oh no, it's not like that. They are just friends, that's all."

"Not according to Ariel. She told her father that Andrew is her boyfriend."

Deputy Jones stood back to gauge the reaction on the woman's face. That would tell her way more about the relationship between the teens than anything she might say to deny it.

Cathi Mosley just looked at the officer blankly before responding. "Well, maybe that's what Ariel thinks, I don't really know. But what I do know is that Andrew doesn't think of her that way. I'm sure of it."

Alicia looked toward the front door. "Is he here?"

"Yes, he's here. But he isn't going to tell you anything differently than what I just told you."

Jones noted the bit of snark in Cathi's voice.

"You never did tell me what you were going to say about Ariel's brother," Cathi stated. "Is he all right?"

"Sean Ford's body was found in the woods." Deputy Jones did her best to show no emotion when delivering the bad news.

Cathi Mosely gasped and her hands flew up to cover her mouth. "Oh my god, what happened?"

"Ma'am, I'm not at liberty to tell you anything about his death. We still have an open investigation pending."

Cathi dropped her hands to her sides. "Oh, of course."

"Where were you four days ago?" Alicia asked.

Cathi's jaw fell open. "What, me? Are you accusing me of something?"

Alicia shook her head. "I'm not accusing anyone of anything. I'm just gathering information at this point."

"Oh."

"So, where were you on the day Ariel and Sean went missing?"

"They both went missing at the same time?"

Alicia shook her head, not doing a very good job of hiding her annoyance. "Ma'am please, just answer my questions, so that we can move the investigation along. Finding Ariel is extremely time sensitive."

Cathi Mosley nodded. "We've been camping for the last week. Down the river a ways, at one of the campgrounds." Cathi pointed in the general direction from where they came.

"Can anyone vouch for you? Did you sign in anywhere? Somewhere we can check?"

Cathi took a deep breath. She didn't like where this line of questioning was going. "Yes, we got a camping permit and checked in at the office. We were at the Serendipity Campground. Is that good enough for you?" She didn't intend on answering in the way it came out, but couldn't help herself.

"You and your children went camping together?"

"Yes."

"Including Andrew?" Alicia asked.

"Oh, well no, it was just me and the girls," Cathi responded.

"Where was Andrew while you were camping?" Alicia asked.

"Do I need a lawyer?" Cathi asked, not answering the question.

"I don't know. Do you?"

CHAPTER 20

The two women stood in silence, staring at each other, for probably a full minute. It seemed like forever to Deputy Jones. But she wasn't about to back down. Something fishy was going on with this family and she needed to find out what it was.

Finally, Cathi Mosley broke the silence. "What exactly is it that you want to know, Deputy?"

Jones took a deep breath. "Since Andrew wasn't with you camping, I want to know where he was. And I want to find out if he knows anything about Ariel's disappearance."

She knew how important it was to not have a contentious relationship with the family. They weren't technically suspected of anything at this point. She was only investigating and asking questions, hoping to find out that 15 year old Andrew was completely innocent, so they could focus their investigation on somebody else. She certainly hoped that he wasn't involved in any way.

Alicia softened her voice. "Look, I'm just trying to get some answers here, so that I can rule Andrew out as a suspect. I'm not trying to pin this on anyone. If he had nothing to do with her disappearance, then let's clear that up now and I can be on my way." Alicia raised her eyebrows. "Okay?"

Cathi nodded. "Yeah, okay." She began walking toward the house. "Come with me."

Alicia followed, dutifully.

The pair found Andrew in the living room, playing a video game on the TV. Cathi walked over and stood in front of her son, effectively blocking his view of the game.

He leaned to his right, trying to get a better view. "Mom, you are in my way. You're gonna get me killed..."

His voice trailed off when he noticed the deputy off to the side.

"Hello, Andrew. I'm Deputy Jones. Got a minute to talk?"

Before answering, he looked over at his mother with wide eyes. She nodded. He did note the sadness on her face.

Turning back to Alicia, Andrew nodded. "Okay sure. What do you want to talk about?"

"Ariel Ford."

"Okay. What about her?"

"You know she's missing, right?" Alicia asked.

"What? No, I didn't know that. Since when?" Andrew asked.

"Since four days ago."

"What? She's been missing for four days and no one told me?"

To Alicia Jones, Andrew did seem sincerely surprised by the news. However, she knew better than to assume that was the case. Some people were good actors. Really good actors.

"It's been all over town," Alicia explained. "Your mother just told me that you didn't go camping with them. So where have you been all this time?"

His eyes flicked to his mother, and back to the deputy. "Um, here."

"Here?" Alicia asked, glancing around the living room. "As in this house? You never left it? Not even once? Not to go see your friends?"

Andrew shook his head. "No, not even once."

He began biting his fingernails. The deputy noticed.

"Have you talked to Ariel in the last few days?"

"No. I texted her, but she never texted me back."

"Did you try calling her?" Alicia asked.

"No."

"Why not?"

Andrew shrugged. "I don't know. I never call anyone. Texting is easier."

Deputy Jones locked eyes with Cathi.

"It's true," his mother confirmed. "He never talks on the phone. Not even with me. Texting is all we can get out of him."

Alicia turned back to the boy. "Is Ariel your girlfriend?"

Andrew looked at his mother once more. She also had a questioning look on her face.

"Don't look at your mother. Look at me," Alicia ordered. "I'm the one asking. It's a simple question. Either she is your girlfriend or she isn't. Which one is it?"

"Um, I didn't do anything."

"I didn't say you did. Answer the question," Alicia repeated.

"Um, sort of? I mean, we hang out and stuff. I know she tells people I'm her boyfriend," Andrew tried to explain.

"Do you correct her when she tells people that?" Alicia asked.

"No. I guess not."

"So, that sounds a lot like she is your girlfriend. That's all I wanted to know. Now was that so difficult?"

"No, I guess not."

"I'm not your enemy here," Alicia continued. "I'm just

trying to find Ariel, that's all. Maybe you know something, maybe you don't. But it all helps in our investigation. She could be in serious danger, and I just want to find her, before the same thing happens to her that happened to her brother."

Andrew's eyes widened like saucers. "What happened to Sean?" He looked back and forth between the women.

"He went missing at the same time as Ariel did and he was killed," Alicia told him.

"Oh my god. Do you think Ariel is dead too?" Andrew asked.

CHAPTER 21

"That's what I'm here trying to prevent. So, next time I ask you a question, can you just give me a straight answer?"

Andrew nodded his head rapidly, his longish hair falling down in front of his eyes. Andrew blew out a puff of air to move it.

The deputy ignored the maneuver. "Good. Now, is there anyone who can verify that you were here at the house for the last four days? Did anyone come over?" Alicia asked. "Anyone at all?"

"Just my friend, Bobby. He came over a few times to play video games. But that's all. I haven't seen anyone else." He glanced over at Cathi. "My mom said it was okay."

Cathi nodded. "That's true."

"Why didn't you answer the phone when we tried calling you?" Alicia asked.

Andrew turned his attention toward the kitchen. "You mean the phone in there? That's my mom's phone. I never answer that."

Jones looked over at Cathi, who nodded. "Also true. He never touches that phone. Like I said, all of our phone

83

contact is by text. I don't know that he even knows the house phone number."

Both women faced the boy. He shrugged.

Jones nodded. Andrew was 15 years old and she knew that what he was saying was probably 100% true. Texting was the way for teenagers these days. If they didn't recognize the phone number, they were never going to answer it. And the fact that Andrew never answered their house phone, because that was his mother's phone, made perfect sense. Alicia herself rarely called anyone, if it wasn't work related.

Andrew looked up at Alicia expectantly. "Deputy?"

"Yes?"

"Can I help look for Ariel? I don't want anything to happen to her. I'm really worried," he told her.

Alicia nodded. "Of course. We will be searching the woods again tomorrow. Go to the trail head parking lot early in the morning and they'll tell you what to do. Do you know where that is?"

"By the river? Yeah I know where it is. I'll be there."

"Okay, I think that's all I need for now," Alicia told mother and son. "I'll contact you if we need anything further. You folks have a good day now."

She cringed a bit with that last statement. She had just told him that his girlfriend was missing and presumed dead. And that Sean's body had already been found. How could they possibly have a good day after that?

But Alicia needed to put that out of her mind as she made her way back to the sheriff's station. There was more to do there. So much more, if they wanted to find the poor girl alive.

CHAPTER 22

Nathan Ford arrived at the search area trailhead long after daybreak. Jake Cavanaugh noted the time on his wristwatch. He watched the father of one dead child, and another who was still missing, come sauntering in hours after everyone else showed up to find *his* children.

Nathan was carrying a white paper cup from a popular local coffee shop. He had about two days worth of beard, and his hair didn't look like it had been brushed in just as long. His gray sweatpants had a small hole in the knee, and his sweatshirt looked as if it had been freshly pulled out of the bottom of his clothes hamper an hour ago.

Were those the telltale signs of a grieving father? Or of a guilty one? That was something Jake Cavanaugh had vowed to find out.

"Hello, Mr. Ford," Jake greeted. "Nice of you to join us."

Deputy Alicia Jones narrowed her eyes at her partner. Jake just shrugged in response. He wasn't wrong, Alicia thought. But she wasn't about to express that out loud, like Jake had.

That was something she had noticed right away about her

new partner. He had no problem saying what was on his mind. She kind of admired that, as she usually didn't have the nerve to do so. But then again, as an officer of the law, he needed some form of a filter on his mouth. It wasn't always wise to say everything that came to mind. Things could be misconstrued, and they could come back to bite them in the ass when called to testify in court.

So yeah, she kept most of her thoughts to herself. It had worked well for her over the years.

"Sorry, I overslept," Nathan responded, not noticing, or maybe not caring, about Jake's snarky tone. "I tossed and turned all night, and finally passed out...er fell asleep around dawn. I'm just glad I didn't sleep all day." He shivered in the cold morning air. "Damn, it's cold out here, don't ya think?" His breath was a misty cloud, with the slightest hint of whiskey.

Both Jake and Alicia caught the slip of the tongue by Nathan, and ignored his feeble attempt to change the subject.

"Have you been drinking, Mr. Ford?" Jake asked.

"Is that against the law now?"

Jake shook his head. "Nope." He pulled out his notepad and began scribbling on it.

"What are you writing?" Nathan asked. "That I showed up drunk? Cause that's none of your business."

Jake looked up, into the man's eyes. "I'm just writing some general notes for myself. Nothing for you to be concerned about."

Nathan let out a huff. "Yeah fine, whatever."

He looked around at all the people milling about in the cold morning air. Some seemed to be checking in. Others were going into the forest, or coming out of it. Not a single one of them appeared as if they had any good news. Or any news at all.

Nathan jumped at the hand that came out of nowhere

from behind and landed on his left shoulder. He dropped his cup of coffee in the dirt at his feet. Barely noticing the splatters on his sweatpants and shoes, Nathan glared at the sheriff standing beside him.

Sheriff Manuel Garcia looked down at the coffee cup lying on the ground, slowly leaking its contents into the dirt.

"Oh hey, sorry about that buddy. But I have a question to ask you," the sheriff announced.

"Yeah, what's that?"

Nathan didn't trust the sheriff one iota. He knew that the man suspected him of killing his wife. He had pretty much said just that. And he probably thought Nathan had strangled his own son too. He clenched at the thought of what the question could possibly be about. Another accusation, he was sure of it.

"Mr. Ford, did you once tell your wife that you didn't want kids?"

CHAPTER 23

Sheriff Garcia released his hold on Nathan's shoulder and crossed his arms, expecting the inevitable 'who me?' argument.

Nathan's chest tightened. "Why would you ask me that?"

There it was. Garcia saw it coming a mile away. Instead of just answering the simple question, Nathan Ford was deflecting. He was probably stalling for time while he figured out how to answer the question without incriminating himself. That's what guilty people did, answering a question with a question.

"Just answer the question, Mr. Ford," Garcia ordered.

"Okay, I will. I have nothing to hide," Nathan told him. "Yes, when Cassandra and I first started dating, I did tell her that. You have to understand, I was very young. Still in college. Having children to care for and raise was a daunting task in my mind. I didn't think it was for me."

"So what changed your mind?"

"Cassandra," he replied without hesitation. "She was so loving and wonderful. And she wanted children. I couldn't imagine my life without her. Therefore I jumped on board.

Now I can't imagine my life without them." Nathan's eyes scanned the area. Sean's face flashed in his mind and his head hung low. "Well, just without Ariel now."

Nathan bit his upper lip in an attempt to stifle the tears that threatened to flow.

Sheriff Garcia, who took his job quite seriously, and rarely believed the lies that came out of a suspect's mouth, was suddenly not so sure about Nathan Ford.

He shook the feeling off. He knew, deep down, that Nathan Ford was the one. The one who killed his wife a year ago, and his son just a few days ago. And, if they weren't already too late, the sheriff's top priority in life at the moment was to make sure Ariel got out of this alive.

"Um, excuse me, where can I find that lady cop?"

"Andrew!" Nathan yelled. "Where the hell is my daughter?" Nathan made a beeline straight for the boy. "You will tell me right now, or I swear I'll…"

Jake Cavanaugh intercepted with a tight grip on the collar of Nathan's sweatshirt before he reached Andrew. "You'll do nothing. And you should watch your threats in front of a bunch of officers, don't you think?"

Nathan Ford's feet just about went out from underneath him when Jake stopped him so abruptly. He hadn't been expecting it and was still moving swiftly when he was pulled to a stop. It took him a moment to get two feet back on solid ground.

"Dammit, man, you almost made me fall." Nathan struggled to get free. "Let me go."

"Are you going to leave the kid alone?" Jake asked, his face deadpanned.

"Yeah, fine." He struggled again. "Turn me loose!"

Jake released his grip on the man's collar. Nathan pulled at and adjusted his shirt, all the while glaring toward Deputy Cavanaugh.

"That kid knows where my daughter is, I just know it. You need to find a way to get it out of him."

"Mr. Ford, shut the hell up," Jake ordered. "We have already questioned him and his mother. They don't know anything."

Nathan caught Andrew's eyes in his own. "Sure they don't."

Andrew put his palms up, facing the men. "I swear, I don't know anything. I didn't even know she was missing until yesterday."

"You're a damn liar!" Nathan screamed.

During all the commotion, Deputy Jones joined the group. "What is going on here?"

"Um Deputy, I came here to talk to you. I wanted to tell you something about Ariel." Andrew glanced over at her father. "In private."

"Anything you have to say about my daughter, you can say right here in front of me and everyone else," Nathan told him.

Deputy Jones could see the trepidation on the boy's face. "Come with me."

Andrew followed her dutifully to the tent a few yards away. Once inside, she pulled the flap down and turned toward him.

"Okay, Andrew, tell me what this is all about."

"Ariel once told me that her father gets violent when he drinks. She was afraid of him."

CHAPTER 24

"Ariel is afraid of her father?" Deputy Jones repeated back what Andrew had just told her.

He nodded and shuffled from foot to foot. "Yeah, and she said it's been getting worse lately. She said he drinks all the time. She hardly ever sees him sober."

The tent flap flew open and Sheriff Garcia stuck his head in. He never did have boundaries when it came to any investigation. "Jones, get out here. We found something."

Alicia and Andrew looked at each other and walked out into the bright sunshine that was starting to warm up the day nicely.

"Young man," Sheriff Garcia directed toward Andrew, "why don't you go see if you can help with the search for Ariel?"

"You didn't find her?" Andrew asked. "I thought you…"

Garcia shook his head. "No, not yet."

Andrew hung his head low. For just a moment he was anticipating that the sheriff would tell them they had found Ariel, alive and well. He looked over at the sheriff and deputy once more, who were both standing near him, watching him in silence. He got the point and wandered toward the forest and the volunteer searchers.

Once Andrew was out of earshot, Alicia asked the sheriff what they had found. She had also hoped for a positive end to the search for Ariel. Jake Cavanaugh joined the pair.

Sheriff Garcia held up a pink bound book. It had a cheap silver lock on it, and said "My Life" on the cover. The lock had been yanked open, probably by the sheriff himself.

Alicia had once been a young teen and recognized it immediately. Her eyes lit up. "That's a diary. Is it Ariel's?"

"Yes. I had Ford's house searched after he left this morning. The diary was found hidden inside a jacket pocket in the back of her closet. I have to admit it was a good hiding place. We missed it the first time, and it was somewhere her father would probably never look."

"That's the sort of place I used to hide my diary in, back in the day."

Alicia smiled at the thought. She wondered what happened to the book that had her innermost teen thoughts written down. It hadn't crossed her mind in years. It was probably in a box in her parents' garage somewhere, along with some of her childhood treasured items. She made a mental note to go dig through their garage when this case was over.

For just a flash Sheriff Garcia considered asking her more about that, but then realized it was the wrong time and place for such a lighthearted discussion.

"So, what's in it?" Jake asked, getting in on the conversation.

"I've only glanced through it so far, but I did find an interesting entry." Garcia opened the diary and flipped to somewhere around three quarters of the way through, and flipped one page at a time. "Okay, here it is. It's from about two weeks ago."

He began reading the diary entry out loud:

I don't know what to do. My dad is always screaming at me. Sean is annoying, and my mother is never coming back. I don't know if I want to stick around. Maybe I'll get on a bus and go far far away. Anywhere would be better than this.

"Do you think she ran away?" Alicia asked.

"Doubtful. I can't imagine that she ran away and Sean died at the same time. There's gotta be more to it than that. Listen to this next entry," Garcia told them.

I hate my dad. I wish he was dead. He hit me last night when he was drunk, for no reason at all. I hate everybody, except Uncle Chris. He is the only one who doesn't treat me like a child. I love him so much.

"Uncle Chris, huh?" Jake exclaimed. "This is disturbing in so many ways. Maybe he knows more about her disappearance than he's telling us."

"Yeah, I don't know about that," Alicia offered. "I used to be a teenage girl and that sounds a lot like she's just being dramatic. I'm sure my diary was full of stuff like that. I remember hating my parents at around that age. It's just the way kids are. Especially young girls."

"What are you saying?" the sheriff asked.

"I'm saying that you shouldn't jump to conclusions. She may have just been venting. Chris probably has no clue about her feelings. Believe me when I say that it's extremely typical for young girls to have new crushes every other week. Even on inappropriate adults."

Sheriff Garcia shook his head. "That's a bunch of hogwash. Where is Chris Ford? I need to have a chat with him."

Deputy Jones slammed her mouth shut and stood in front of the sheriff without saying another word. Having the sheriff just dismiss her contribution to the case was demoralizing. She had legitimate information that could help with insight into the mind of a 13 year old girl. Her own personal experience was important. In a station full of mostly men, Alicia had learned to stand up for herself. But this time felt differently. Sheriff Garcia didn't even take one moment out of his day to consider that what she was telling them might be somewhat useful.

Deputy Jones spun on her heels and headed back to the tent. Closing the flap behind her, as she needed a few minutes alone. Pacing back and forth from one end of the tent to the other, she cursed the sheriff under her breath.

It was just something she needed to do at the moment. She knew that once her little tantrum was over, she would be fine, and things would go back to normal. Until the next time, that is. But she couldn't worry about that. Right now, she needed to focus on finding the missing girl. If Ariel Ford was truly out in the woods, and still alive, she wouldn't be that way for long.

CHAPTER 25

"Chris is over there with his brother," Jake pointed out. He had noticed Alicia walk away, and she looked angry. But he couldn't focus on that at the moment.

Sheriff Garcia turned in the direction Jake was pointing. Nathan and Chris appeared to be deep in conversation. He stood watching them for a moment. They almost seemed to be having a fun, light-hearted time. It was beyond the comprehension of the sheriff that a man with a missing wife, a dead son, and a missing daughter, could be having a good time at the search site of his daughter.

When Nathan threw his head back and howled with laughter, following something his brother said, that was it. He was going to get to the bottom of Nathan and Chris' involvement in the family's tragedies, no matter how he went about making that happen.

"Let's go." Garcia covered the distance in seconds. Jake followed.

Nathan noticed him first.

"I like a good laugh. What's so funny over here?" Garcia asked.

Nathan looked at his brother. "What do you mean?"

"Something pretty amusing was going on between you two. I could hear you howling from over at the tent. So... what was so amusing?"

Nathan shrugged. "Nothing. Chris here was just making a joke. It was stupid. I don't know why I even laughed. I think the stress of this whole situation is getting to me." Nathan looked around at all the curious faces watching their interaction.

"Yeah, it was not even that funny," Chris added. "But I agree, this is probably not the place for it."

"*Probably* not the place?" Garcia asked.

Chris averted his eyes. "Sorry."

Nathan cut in. "Sheriff, did you find anything out about my daughter?"

Garcia ignored Nathan, instead he turned to his brother. "I would like to know what was going on between you and your niece." It came out as more of an accusation than a question.

Chris' eyes went wide. "What are you talking about, Sheriff? Nothing was going on...if you mean what I think you mean."

Garcia interrupted him, mid-sentence. "You know exactly what I mean. She wrote in her diary about how you are the only one who doesn't treat her like a child and how much she loves you. Now what exactly do you think that is about?"

During the exchange between the sheriff and Chris Ford, Nathan stood to the side, conspicuously quiet.

"It's not about anything. I'm her uncle, and that is all." Chris turned to his brother. "Nathan, I would never...I mean, that's just...I swear, nothing at all was going on." It seemed that Chris couldn't form a coherent sentence on the matter.

"Do you think we are new at this, Mr. Ford?" Sheriff Garcia addressed Chris. He didn't wait for a response. "The answer is no. I've been in law enforcement for more than thirty years. And believe me, when I tell you that I've seen it all. I have spent most of those years chasing a serial killer." His eyes flicked over to Jake Cavanaugh. Jake averted his eyes.

The sheriff continued. "A grown man having a thing, or fling, or whatever you want to call it, with a thirteen year old girl, is nothing new. And unfortunately, it's not even that shocking anymore. So, I'm going to ask you again, what is going on between the two of you?"

Nathan still had not reacted. His eyes bore into his brother. Everyone was so focused on Chris at the moment, that no one had noticed.

"I already answered you. Nothing. Absolutely nothing like that was going on between us. She's my niece. I love her. We have a normal uncle, niece relationship and nothing else. End of story."

"Is it the end of the story though?" Garcia asked, not believing a word the man told him.

"Yes." He turned to Nathan. "Bro, you have to believe me. I can't help it if your daughter had a little crush on me."

"What the hell did you just say?" Nathan responded with clenched teeth. His arms remained hanging at his side, fists clenched.

"There it is," Garcia jumped in. "So there was something happening. Mr. Ford, give me your phone. I bet we are going to find a whole lot more than a little crush, aren't we?"

Chris' eyebrows shot up. "What? Why do you need my phone?"

"Because if anything was going on, there's always evidence on the phone. Always. People are pretty stupid when it comes to their phones. You all really have no clue what treasure troves of evidence we can uncover. They are usually full of calls, texts, emails, photos..." He dragged out that last word, knowing that the photos were what got most people into trouble. God, people were stupid.

Garcia reached out his hand and held it there between them. He and Chris locked eyes for just a second.

Chris looked down at the outstretched palm and then glanced at those standing around. "It's not what it looks like."

"And what does it look like, Mr. Ford?" Garcia asked.

"The stuff on my phone is nothing, I swear," Chris added, ignoring the sheriff's question.

"It's always what it looks like," the sheriff responded.

"What's on your phone, Chris?" Nathan asked, barely able to get the words out.

Chris looked over at his brother and the pair locked eyes. He dropped his gaze to the dirt beneath his feet almost instantly.

What his brother was about to find out might shock his world. Chris knew that, and also knew that it would be difficult to explain the texts and photos on his phone. Though he had deleted them all, he was bright enough to know that nothing was truly gone. The cops would have no trouble finding them.

He cursed himself for not having the forethought to destroy his phone the moment that Ariel went missing. He was afraid that he would live to regret that oversight.

"It wasn't me, Nathan. It was all Ariel. Every bit of it," Chris responded, without looking up.

CHAPTER 26

"That sounds a lot like victim blaming," Jake Cavanaugh interrupted.

Deputy Alicia Jones had calmed down enough, after her disagreement with the sheriff, and joined them, mid-discussion. The air was tense, and no one even gave her a passing glance.

"Hand the phone over, Mr. Ford. I'm not going to ask you again," Sheriff Garcia told him in slow, deliberate terms.

Alicia looked between the men. Clearly, she had missed something. She looked to Jake for clarification, but he just shook his head. Okay, now was not the time for explanations. She would just have to wait and see how this played out.

Chris knew that the sheriff probably needed a search warrant to take his phone. But he also knew that if he argued about it, he would only be postponing the inevitable. They would get his phone, whether he liked it or not. Based on Ariel's diary entries, they would be able to get that search warrant and there was nothing he could do about it.

Chris reached into his jacket pocket and pulled out his

cell phone, hesitating only an instant before dropping it into the waiting palm of the sheriff. Garcia immediately passed it along to Deputy Jones, who put it in a plastic evidence bag. There was always a stash of them in her jacket pocket.

"Get that to processing immediately," he told Alicia. "I want to know what's on there within the hour. Got it?"

Alicia very much doubted it would happen that fast. But she wasn't about to argue with the boss. "Yeah, got it." She took off toward her waiting patrol car.

Sheriff Garcia turned back to the brothers. "I think the two of you need to come on down to the station while we wait for the results." His next statement was directed right at Chris Ford. "Since you've already made it really clear that there is something on your phone we aren't going to like, I don't see any reason to hang around here in the meantime. Do you?"

Chris averted his eyes and ran his fingers through his full head of blond hair. "No, I guess not."

Nathan Ford desired nothing more at that moment than to avoid the sheriff's station. "Shouldn't I stay here and help look for Ariel?"

Sheriff Garcia made a dramatic show of scanning the area. "Mr. Ford, what do you see before you?"

Nathan looked around. "Um, I don't know. Maybe a hundred people wandering around?"

"They aren't wandering, Mr. Ford, they are searching for your daughter. If she's out there, we will find her. You can count on that."

"What do you mean, *if* she's out there? Where else could she be?"

Garcia hesitated for a moment. "It's a big world out there, Mr. Ford. She could be just about anywhere. But, due to the fact that we found your son in the area, I'm willing to bet that your daughter is also nearby."

Nathan didn't want to think about exactly what those words meant.

Sheriff Garcia wasn't expecting to find Ariel Ford alive. Oh, he very much hoped he was wrong. He would be thrilled if they found her alive and well, just hanging out at a friend's house, but he didn't expect that to be the case at all.

It was pretty rare to find a missing child alive after the first couple of days. And at this point, they had been looking for her for five days. If she was in the forest, it seemed quite unlikely that she could survive on her own. And if she were with the kidnapper, her chances were even slimmer. Poor Sean hadn't made it more than 24 hours.

It was likely that Ariel had met the same fate.

The sheriff wanted to keep as close an eye on Nathan Ford and his brother as possible. Someone was lying to him, hell they probably both were, and he needed to get those answers as quickly as possible.

Sheriff Garcia grasped Jake's shoulder. "Deputy Cavanaugh here will be happy to give you both a ride to the station. Won't you, Deputy?"

"Of course. Come on, gentlemen." Jake led them to a waiting car.

Alicia accompanied the trio, after speaking briefly with the sheriff.

Once they reached the sheriff's station, Deputies Jones and Cavanaugh escorted them inside. The sheriff had instructed them to put the brothers in an interrogation room together. It was not their usual way of doing things. Normally suspects are questioned separately. But Sheriff Garcia frequently did things his own way. The rules be damned.

The Black River Killer case was the perfect example of the sheriff's unorthodox investigation methods.

It wasn't so long ago that Sheriff Garcia caught the Black River Killer. She was someone who had been killing the citizens of Black River for over thirty years. He had taken a lot of heat for not being able to solve the case for so long. But once she was arrested, and everyone knew who the killer was, they could understand why it had been so difficult for the sheriff's department to solve.

Leigh Cavanaugh, Deputy Jake Cavanaugh's mother, turned out to be the one. Everyone who knew her was astonished when her identity was revealed. They all knew her as a good mom to her two children, a friendly neighbor, and just an overall nice person.

Not a single person in town could think of any specific instance in all the years they had known her, where she showed any inkling that she was a cold blooded killer.

In fact, she had been killing since she was only six years old. That was what shocked everyone the most. It was almost beyond comprehension that a six year old could kill and remain undetected for decades. But she did, and she was.

Though Sheriff Manuel Garcia got the credit for apprehending the Black River Killer, it was actually the killer's son, Jake, who solved the case. Even though he was only a teenager at the time.

A book was published about the case, called The Dark Years. There probably wasn't a citizen of Black River who hadn't read it.

And everyone had an opinion about it.

Sheriff Garcia had made a few enemies during his investigation of that case. He wasn't happy about that fact, as they all lived in the same small town, but it came with the territory.

CHAPTER 27

Brothers, Nathan and Chris, were left alone in the interrogation room. That was by design. The camera focused squarely on them might tell the investigators something that the brothers would never reveal on purpose.

Chris was the one who noticed the camera the moment they walked in. He stood and stared at it for a moment. Then he turned to his brother, and without saying a word, gave a quick nod of his head in the direction of that upper corner of the room. Nathan's eyes locked on the camera in response. Neither brother sat. Both were too nervous to do so, and went to their respective corners of the small room.

Nathan didn't care if the camera was there or not, and he certainly didn't care who was watching. All he cared about at the moment was his daughter. He needed answers from his brother about the relationship between him and Ariel. And he needed the answers now.

Nathan spoke first. "We need to talk, be damned the camera." He glanced up at it once more. "Is there something I should know about you and my daughter?" Nathan directed at his younger brother. "And don't lie to me."

"What? No. I told you there isn't. She is just a kid. And she's my niece. So, no. Absolutely not." Chris punctuated his words by waving his arms in the air. "I can't believe you are actually asking me that. What do you expect me to say? That we were fooling around? Ew, gross. That's just...I mean, ew." His face scrunched up in disgust as he spoke.

Chris looked up at the air vent above their heads. "Damn, it's hot in here." He raised his voice and looked directly at the camera. "Can you guys turn on the air?" He pulled at his collar. "It's a sauna in here."

The officers watching the monitor looked at each other and smiled, ignoring his request. They liked it when their suspects were a bit uncomfortable. It made them more eager to get on with it and out of the hot, or cold, room.

"You might as well tell me what they are going to find on your phone," Nathan said, keeping his voice as calm as he possibly could. "It's all going to come out anyway."

"Can we get some water in here?" Chris said directly to the camera. "I'm gonna pass out if you don't do something!"

Still...no response.

Chris ran his fingers through his blond hair and glanced once more at the camera up in the corner, before fixing his gaze down at the table in front of him.

"Chris?"

"Yeah, yeah, all right. But before I tell you, you have to promise me that you won't freak out. Okay?"

"This is my daughter we are talking about. And she's missing. And you are starting to look really bad in this situation. So no, I'm not promising you anything. Just tell me," Nathan ordered.

The two brothers, still in opposite corners of the room, stared at each other in silence.

"Now Chris!"

"Ariel has a crush on me," Chris blurted out, without looking his brother in the eyes.

"Yes, that is something we already know. What we don't know is what you did about that."

Chris looked into his brother's eyes. "Nothing! I did absolutely nothing about it. I swear, it's the truth."

"You didn't encourage her at all?" Nathan asked.

"No. Why would I do that?"

"Oh I don't know. It's not like your morals are all filled with good intentions. You did sleep with my wife after all."

Chris averted his eyes.

"You got nothing to say about that?" Nathan asked.

"Look, I know that was wrong. It was a mistake, and if I could change things, I would. But I can't. So that's something I'll have to live with. I hurt you, and for that I'm deeply sorry."

Nathan could see the regret in his little brother's eyes. Even still, it would be a long time before he could forgive him for what he had done. And if he had anything inappropriate going on with Ariel, Nathan would not only never forgive Chris, he would kill him.

Ignoring the apology, Nathan pressed on. "So, what's on your phone, Chris?"

"It's nothing. Really."

"So tell me and stop jerking me around," Nathan pressed.

Chris gave in. "All right, all right. Ariel texted me some photos of herself."

Nathan stood in that same spot, back straight as a board, and silent for almost a full minute, unable to speak.

"Did you hear me?"

"Yeah, I heard you," Nathan responded. "What...kind...of photos?" He could barely get the words out. He was sure he already knew the answer, but needed to hear it out loud.

"The second I saw them, I deleted them. I swear."

"What kind of photos, Chris?"

Chris backed as far into the corner as he could get. "Nude photos. I'm sorry."

CHAPTER 28

Suddenly Nathan couldn't breathe. He bent over, trying to get some air. What little air he could get came in shuddering gasps. It felt like he was dying. He shivered, even as sweat dripped from his nose, landing in tiny drops onto the floor in front of his face. He stared at them as he continued trying to catch his breath.

"Are you all right?" Chris asked. "Should I call someone?" He walked over and patted Nathan on the back.

Nathan stood straight up once more, flinging Chris' hand off of him. "Don't touch me!" He turned to face his little brother. "I'll never forgive you for this."

"It's not my fault! I didn't encourage her in any way, I swear. It was all her."

"Did you take my daughter?"

"No, of course not, Nathan. I would never do that. I love her." Chris thought about what he had just said, and quickly added to it. "Like a niece, that's all."

"And what about my wife, and my son? Did you kill them too?"

Chris' eyes grew wide. "I didn't take or kill anyone. I wouldn't do that. You have to believe me."

Nathan paced a circle inside the square interrogation room. "I don't know what to believe at this point. All I know is that Cassandra and Ariel have gone missing and you were involved with both of them."

"I was never involved with Ariel. That's just wrong. Stop saying that." Chris' words were low and calm. He wasn't sure that he had any fight left in him.

"Wrong? That didn't stop you from sleeping with my wife."

Chris took an exasperated breath. "Look, that was a long time ago. I've apologized, and really do regret it. Can we just move on? I don't know anything about where she is. And yes, getting involved with Ariel is worlds apart from my relationship with Cassandra. At least we were consenting adults. Ariel is thirteen. That's just incomprehensible."

"So, what do you think?" Sheriff Garcia asked Jake, as they watched the two brothers from the next room. Jones had gone back to the search site to keep an eye on things. So far...nothing.

"I think one or both of them is lying to us. And have been all along. I can't see someone else being involved. They have both either lost their minds, or they are working together. This whole thing could be them playing it up for the camera," Jake told him.

Sheriff Garcia nodded slowly. "That's an interesting take. I still think that Nathan Ford is the guilty one here. I think that Chris got caught up in it all when he decided to bed his brother's wife. It seems unlikely to me that he would do anything to the wife or the daughter. I don't see any motive here. Do you?"

"Actually, yes. Chris was sleeping with Cassandra. Maybe she threatened to tell her husband. That would have been catastrophic to the relationship between the brothers, and the family as a whole, don't you think?"

Garcia nodded.

Jake continued. "He could have killed her to shut her up. Cassandra wasn't important to him, but his brother may have been."

"How important could his brother have been to him if Chris was sleeping with his wife?" Garcia asked.

"I think it's complicated," Jake replied. "And I think it's entirely possible that Chris felt remorse for the whole thing. The only way he could make it go away was to get rid of the evidence."

"Cassandra was the evidence?" the sheriff asked.

Jake nodded. "Yep."

"Okay, not a bad theory," Garcia told him. "But why the daughter? Other than the fact that she had a crush on her uncle, why would he feel the need to get rid of her?"

"Oh, that's an easy one," Jake told him.

CHAPTER 29

Sheriff Garcia looked Jake Cavanaugh in the eyes. "Chris killing his niece is an easy one?"

"Sure. Don't you see it? He just admitted that she sent him nude photos. She's thirteen. That could get him a lot of years in prison. He knew that deleting the photos wouldn't make any difference. If anyone...ever...found out about it, he would be done for," Jake explained.

"And he couldn't take that chance," Jake continued. "Ariel is very young, and very naive, I'm sure. She could easily have told her friends about the photos. Hell, they probably already know. Once that happened, it would be out there in the world. There would be no way to contain the story. Chris knew that. It's the perfect motive to shut her up permanently."

"That's an excellent point," Garcia admitted. "Now, how are we going to prove it?"

"Sheriff, we found something on Ford's phone."

Garcia and Jake turned to face the tech.

"We already know what's on there," Sheriff Garcia responded. "Nude photos of Ariel Ford."

The tech nodded. "Yes, but that's not all."

"Tell us," Garcia ordered.

The tech smiled. "Even better, I'll play it for you. It's a voicemail that Ariel left for her uncle." The tech pressed play.

'Uncle Chris, you have to get over here. My dad is drunk again. He's freaking out and he hit Sean.'

Both men's eyes grew wide when they heard Nathan Ford in the background screaming. Then, another voice.

"No!"

Sheriff Garcia put up his hand and the tech pressed the stop button.

"Was that Sean who yelled 'no' on the recording?" he asked.

"I'm sure it was," the tech answered. "Do you want to hear the rest of it?"

Garcia nodded.

They could hear Nathan Ford's voice growing louder and louder as he screamed obscenities at his children.

"Oh god, here he comes. Uncle Chris, please help us! We need..."

The phone went dead. The recording had stopped in the middle of Ariel's plea.

Sheriff Garcia thought about the recording for a moment before speaking. He spoke directly to the technician holding the phone. "When was that voicemail left?"

"Three days before she was reported missing."

"Okay, thank you. Make copies of everything you find on that phone," Garcia ordered.

"Already done."

"Okay good. Give me the phone."

The tech handed the phone to the sheriff, turned and walked out.

"Now what?" Jake asked the sheriff.

"Now we go have a talk with the brothers."

"Both of them? Is that the wise thing to do?" Jake knew

that it was unusual to keep both of them in one room, giving them a chance to get their stories straight. But to question them together? It seemed like a really bad idea to him.

"Yes. Both of them."

The brothers turned toward the sound as the door to the interrogation room squeaked opened.

"Sheriff, when are we getting out of here?" Chris Ford asked.

"I don't have an answer to that, just yet. We have things to talk to you about, and it may take a while. I would get comfortable, if I were you," he responded, indicating the table and chairs.

"So, while you are here harassing us," Nathan jumped in, "who is out there looking for my daughter?"

"Oh, you don't need to worry about that. The search for Ariel is still in full swing."

"So why do you have us in here?" Nathan added.

"You know why," Jake answered. "Because of your brother's relationship with your daughter."

All eyes turned toward Chris.

Chris' eyes grew wide. "There is no relationship, Deputy. At least there's nothing more than an uncle and niece relationship. That's it. That's all there has ever been."

"I don't believe you," Jake stated with a deadpan face. "Teen girls don't send nude photos of themselves to their uncles if there isn't something going on. Did you touch her when she was a little girl?"

"I'm going to kill you!" Chris ran at the deputy.

Surprisingly to everyone, Nathan was the one who intercepted his brother. Chris stopped abruptly when Nathan stepped in front of Jake. Nathan stuck his chest out. He wasn't about to back down. Jake moved out of the line of fire.

"This isn't helping," Nathan told him. "All I care about right now is finding Ariel. We can deal with your relationship, or whatever you want to call it, later." His words were said through clenched teeth. It was all he could do not to tear his brother's throat out right there in front of everyone. "But I'm telling you right now, if I find out there is anything to the deputy's accusations, I will kill you myself."

Nathan didn't care at all that the sheriff and the deputy were standing right there when he made the threat. He meant every word of it. If his brother had touched his daughter, that would be the end of him. And if Nathan had to spend the rest of his life in prison for it, so be it.

"Gentlemen, gentlemen," Sheriff Garcia intercepted, "let's all calm down now. This is getting us nowhere." He put a hand on Nathan's shoulder and guided him back a few feet. "Now, that's better. Can we have an adult conversation now?"

Secretly, Sheriff Garcia enjoyed the show. The riff between the brothers gave them way more information about who they were than any questions ever would. Both Nathan and Chris were hot heads, that part was clear. But actually being capable of killing two children? And a wife? Well, that was to be determined. Either way, it was the duty of the sheriff to find out the answer to those questions.

"We found more than pictures on your phone, Chris," Sheriff Garcia announced.

CHAPTER 30

"We have a recording of a voicemail that we got off of Chris' phone here," the sheriff explained.

"From who?" Nathan was almost afraid to hear the answer.

"From none other than your thirteen year old daughter."

Nathan's eyes narrowed. "Ariel? What does it say?"

Without another word, Garcia pressed play.

Sheriff Garcia, Deputy Jake Cavanaugh, Nathan and Chris Ford all stood in silence as it played.

Nathan's breathing became labored at the sound of him screaming obscenities at his children, and Sean yelling 'No!' in the background. Not to mention Ariel's pleas for help from her uncle.

Once the phone went dead and the recording stopped, Nathan bent over with his hands on his knees. If he didn't get his breathing under control, he would pass out for sure. Everyone watched him closely. His face went pale and once again sweat slid down the side of his face, drip, drip, dripping onto the dirty white tiles beneath him.

No one moved as they watched him.

After a few minutes, Nathan stood upright, slowly. The tension in the room was palpable as the father's primal screams echoed through the sterile walls of the interrogation room. The officers exchanged worried glances, unsure of how to handle the situation.

They had seen their fair share of outbursts, but something about this one felt different. The man's eyes were wide with fear and confusion, and his body was shaking with an intensity that made it difficult to keep him restrained.

Jake stepped forward, trying to speak calmly over the father's screams. "Sir, we need you to calm down. We just want to know what happened to your daughter."

Nathan's screams turned into sobs as he collapsed onto the ground. "I don't remember," he cried. "I don't remember that day. I don't remember anything."

They shared another glance, knowing that this was not the first time they had heard a suspect claim memory loss. But something about the father's demeanor felt genuine, and they decided to pursue the lead.

"Chris, you are free to go. For now," Sheriff Garcia announced.

"But, but...what about Nathan? Should we take him to a hospital?" Chris asked. Genuine concern for his big brother was evident on his face.

"Your brother will be fine. We need to speak to him alone."

Chris still hadn't moved.

Sheriff Garcia looked him dead in the eyes. "Right now, Mr. Ford. If you don't leave right now, you can be our guest in the cell down the hall for the night. Which will it be?"

Chris Ford hesitated for only a moment longer. "I'm not going anywhere. Someone needs to be here to make sure my brother is treated fairly. You can deal with me, or I can call a lawyer. Which will it be?"

Sheriff Garcia had been thankful that Nathan had not asked for an attorney up until this point. He didn't want to press his luck, so he relented. "Yeah, fine. You can stay, but stay out of the way. Got it?"

Chris nodded.

～

The sheriff questioned Nathan for hours, trying once again to piece together the events of the night Ariel Ford disappeared. Nathan's memories were sporadic, at best. Chris sat silently the entire time.

But as the hours wore on, Nathan's denial only fueled their suspicion, and they continued to press him for answers. He insisted that he had no idea where his daughter could be, but the detectives knew there was more to the story.

The door to the interrogation room opened and in stepped Deputy Jones. She motioned for the sheriff and Jake to join her outside the room.

Once all three were in the hallway, she leaned in, so as to not alert anyone who might be within earshot. "I was just notified by the forensic team that they have confirmed the footprints out in the forest around where Sean's body was found, definitely belonged to his father."

Sheriff Garcia nodded and all three stepped into the interrogation room where Nathan Ford waited.

"Mr. Ford," Sheriff Garcia looked at the brothers, "We have conclusively identified the shoe prints out in the forest around where we found Sean's body. They are yours."

CHAPTER 31

Nathan Ford's face turned a deep shade of red as he tried to process what the Sheriff had just said. His mind was racing as he tried to come up with a plausible explanation for why his shoe prints had been found at the scene of the crime.

"I swear to you, Sheriff, I had nothing to do with Sean's death," Nathan pleaded, his voice cracking with emotion.

"I'm sorry, Mr. Ford, but the evidence doesn't lie," the sheriff replied sternly. "We also have eyewitness accounts from several hikers who saw you in the area around the time that Sean was killed."

Nathan's mind was in a blur as he tried to remember where he had been around the day of Sean's disappearance. He had been out hiking in the forest, the day before he found them missing. But he couldn't remember exactly where he had been or how long he had stayed out. He knew how it would sound. He would sound like a guilty man if he said he was casually out hiking.

No one had noticed how quiet Chris Ford was. He was pressing himself into the wall as closely as he could get. He had been accused of atrocities that he couldn't even fathom.

"I can't explain the shoe prints, Sheriff, but I swear to you I had nothing to do with Sean's death," Nathan tried to explain, once again.

"The forensics say differently. No one here is going to believe a word you say if you keep lying to us," Garcia said. "So why are your shoe prints near where we found Sean's body?"

"I...I...I was out...hiking. That's all," Nathan managed to choke out.

The laugh escaped Deputy Cavanaugh's face before he had the chance to stifle it. "Hiking? That's your story?" Jake asked. "Somehow, you don't strike me as the hiking type."

Nathan's heart began to race. He needed to think of something fast or he would end up spending the rest of his life in prison. He couldn't let that happen. If Ariel was still alive, he had so much to live for. He took a deep breath and tried to keep his voice steady.

"Look, Sheriff, I know how it looks, but please, just hear me out. I was out there on the day of the murder, but I wasn't alone. I had met someone, a woman, and we ended up spending the day together. We hiked and talked and..." Nathan trailed off, not wanting to reveal too much.

"A woman?" the sheriff raised an eyebrow. "Who is this woman? And why is this the first time we are hearing this? Does she have a name?"

Nathan hesitated, he wasn't sure if he should say her name or not. But he knew he had no choice. He needed to clear his name.

"Her name is Emma, Emma Sanderson, I think. We met at a bar a few days ago.

"You think? You don't know for sure what her name is?"

"Yeah, I'm pretty sure it's Sanderson. I know her first name is Emma. We only met that one time. After that, well you know, this all happened," Nathan told them with a wave of his hand. "I honestly don't remember much from that day."

The sheriff turned to Jake. "Cavanaugh, find this Emma person and get her in here. We need to have a chat."

Jake nodded and left the room. No one spoke until the door closed behind him.

"So," Sheriff Garcia turned back to Nathan, "tell us more about these memory lapses of yours. When did the blackouts start?"

Nathan shifted from foot to foot, taking in his words. The sheriff jotted down a few notes on his pad, then looked back up at the man. "And how often do these blackouts occur?"

"Maybe once or twice a week," he replied.

The sheriff leaned forward, his eyes searching Nathan's. "And have you ever considered that there might be something more going on here? That perhaps these blackouts are not just a result of alcohol, but rather a symptom of something deeper?"

Nathan furrowed his brow, confused. "What do you mean?"

"Well," Garcia began, "sometimes blackouts can be a sign of dissociation. Have you ever felt like you weren't really in control of your actions during one of these episodes?"

He thought for a moment, then slowly nodded. "Yeah, actually. There have been times where it's like I'm watching myself from outside of my body."

The sheriff nodded, jotting down more notes.

Deputy Jones tilted her head at the sheriff and confusion clouded her face. She leaned in. "Since when are you a therapist?"

Garcia smiled. "You don't know everything about me."

The sheriff knew that Nathan was full of it. He was just reacting to Garcia prompting him with alternate versions of reality. Nathan jumped on it, just as Garcia knew he would. At this point, Nathan would do just about anything, and say just about anything to get himself out of the jam he had found himself in.

CHAPTER 32

The sheriff turned to Alicia. "Jones, get his complete statement on camera." He pointed toward Nathan Ford.

"What about his brother?" she asked.

Garcia regarded Chris. "He can go for now. But keep an eye on him." He made sure to say all of it so that Chris would hear it loud and clear.

The deputy headed out the door.

Alicia returned not a full minute later and commenced with getting Nathan's videotaped statement.

As they left the interrogation room, Jake Cavanaugh caught up with Garcia and Alicia. "I found Emma Sanderson. Nathan was right about her name."

"Are you going out to see her?" the sheriff asked.

"No, I've already spoken with her on the phone. She said they met in a bar and were together in the forest for a bit that night. She said that she didn't know anything about Sean or a body. They just hooked up. That was it. Then they went their separate ways. That's all she knows," Jake explained. "She hasn't spoken with him since."

"All right," Garcia responded. "Keep her info, just in case I have more questions."

"I never thought we'd be dealing with something like this in our small town," Jake muttered.

Sheriff Garcia stopped, dead in his tracks, and slid his eyes toward Jake. "You're familiar with the Black River Killer, right? The very one who terrorized our town for about thirty years?"

Jake stared at the floor. He knew the point that the sheriff was trying to make. Jake's own mother was none other than the Black River Killer. She had killed dozens of people, before Jake figured it out. He was the one responsible for her finally being caught.

"Yeah. I just meant..." It was the only response Jake could come up with.

"I know what you meant." For a moment there, Garcia imagined what it must be like for Jake to be the son of a notorious killer. He never really thought of killers as having families that loved them. But of course they did. Funny how that fact had escaped him.

Chris Ford couldn't get out of the sheriff's station fast enough. He blew past the sheriff and Jake like his feet were on fire.

"Oh hey, Mr. Ford?" the sheriff called out from behind him.

Chris stopped, looked to the ceiling, took a deep breath, and turned around to face the officers. Dammit, he hadn't been fast enough.

"I remember you saying in passing the other day that you and your family went camping in the woods a lot when you were children. Is there a particular area of the woods that you would go?" Garcia asked.

Chris was not a stupid man, recent events not withstanding, he knew exactly where the sheriff was going with that question. But truth be told, he didn't care. He knew in his heart that he had nothing to do with the disappearance of his niece and nephew. He couldn't imagine that Nathan did either. But if he did, Chris wanted to make sure that Nathan paid for it. He would not stand by a killer. Brother or not.

They had already lost Sean, and Chris loved them both. He didn't know if his heart could take it if anything happened to Ariel also. Even if he was never allowed to see her again. It didn't matter. As long as she was safe, that's all that he cared about.

"Mr. Ford?" the sheriff prompted.

"Oh sorry. Um, yeah, we usually stayed in the camp-ground down by the river. I think it was called 'River Heights' or something like that.

"I know it," Jake told them. "It's not far from where we have the search command set up at the trailhead."

Chris pointed at them. "Yep, that's the one. Anything else? No offense, but I'd really like to get out of here." He gave them a slight smile.

They understood.

CHAPTER 33

The searchers wasted no time in grabbing their gear and heading out into the rain. The darkness was palpable, the only light coming from their flashlights and the occasional bolt of lightning illuminating the sky. They trudged through the mud, branches and leaves crunching underfoot.

As the search party combed the woods, the rain continued to pour, drenching everyone to the bone. The flashlights illuminated the dense foliage, casting eerie shadows on the trees. It was a nightmare come to life, and the longer they searched, the more hopeless it seemed.

Deputy Alicia Jones was in charge of the search. She was freezing and miserable. Her stomach growled after hours of searching without stopping for a break.

None of it mattered. They were not going to stop until they searched every inch of those woods, even if it took a week. She wasn't about to let the same monster who had strangled Sean, get his sister also. That family wouldn't be able to survive another tragedy.

Something glimmered in the brush. The part-time officer could barely believe his eyes. In the darkness and rain, there had been just enough moonlight fighting its way through, that it reached something there in front of him.

He bent over and brushed away pine needles and other forest debris, picking it up. He discovered that it was a cell phone lying on the ground, abandoned and forgotten.

"Deputy!" he called.

Alicia was about twenty yards ahead of him, and turned at the sound of his voice.

"I found something!" he yelled over the din of the rain.

The group of searchers all gathered around the officer, who was holding up the phone like a prize he had just won.

It was a crucial clue, and it sent a ripple of excitement through the group.

Deputy Jones took the phone and carefully examined it, checking for any signs of the missing girl. Any sort of clue as to where Ariel might be would be welcomed. It still worked. That was a miracle. As she scrolled through the messages, she stumbled upon a conversation between Ariel and an unknown number.

The messages were cryptic and vague, but it was clear that she had arranged to meet someone in the woods that night. The officer's heart sank as she realized that Ariel may have willingly put herself in danger.

She knew the kind of person who would meet a 13 year old girl in the woods in the middle of the night. Other than the small possibility that a group of friends wanted to get together and drink, whoever set up the meeting was probably up to no good.

They had questioned her friends at length, and were pretty certain it was none of them. Impressing upon them that telling the truth was much more important than getting into a bit of trouble, she felt that none of them were lying.

That left one possibility that she could imagine. A predator.

And the fact that Ariel never returned, cemented that theory.

As the rain continued to pour down on the cops searching the woods, a sense of dread washed over them. The cell phone they had found was the only lead they had, and it really was not of much help. Alicia called into the station to trace the number of the person who had been texting with Ariel.

Within minutes, they called back that it was an untrace-able burner phone.

"Damn. Okay, find out where that phone was purchased, and if there is any video footage of the purchase. It isn't much, but we might get lucky."

She hung up her cell phone, that she had to keep under her rain jacket. She had hoped to get something from the trace, but no such luck.

Things seemed to be going from bad to worse.

"Hey look." Everyone turned to see where the officer was pointing.

In front of them stood a small cabin tucked away in a remote corner of the woods. It was dilapidated and looked as if it was being held up by glue and sticks.

A noise from inside caught their attention. One of the officers aimed his flashlight toward the sound and saw what he thought was a figure behind a broken window inside.

He couldn't see the person, if that's what it truly was that he saw, very clearly. The figure peering at them from the filth covered window looked to be about the size of a 13 year old girl. It really was hard to tell in the rain, and through a dirty, broken window.

"Someone's inside," he called. "It might be her."

CHAPTER 34

The searchers rushed toward the cabin. Deputy Jones held up her hands in a stopping motion.

"Okay everyone, I know you are excited to find the girl, but we need to be cautious here. Let's not overwhelm her... or whoever that is inside, by all rushing in at once. I'll go in first and assess the situation."

"Are you sure it's a good idea to go in alone?" one of the officers questioned. "What if there are more people inside and someone is armed?"

Alicia tilted her head, contemplating the question. He was right. Though it seemed unlikely. She thought for a moment. Was it unlikely? If the girl had been abducted, and dragged out to this remote cabin, there probably was someone inside with her.

It could be dangerous just walking in, expecting only Ariel. If she wasn't alone, that person was probably armed. And hell, they didn't even know if she was in there at all.

It could be suicide going in without backup.

Alicia pointed at the officer who had questioned her. "You. Come with me. The rest of you, secure the perimeter."

They both pulled out their guns and cautiously approached the cabin. Without taking her eyes off the task in front of her, Alicia could hear the stealthy footsteps of her officers crunching through the soggy forest debris, as they made their way around the outside.

Pressing her ear to the front door, she heard nothing. No one talking, no one moving, no one breathing. Had the officer imagined that he saw someone inside? Very possibly. They all so much wanted to find Ariel alive, that she wouldn't be surprised if he had just seen a shadow moving from a flashlight and surmised what was inside from that.

Either way, they needed to find out. If Ariel was still alive, she might not be for much longer. She was young and probably without food and water. If it was her inside at all.

Alicia led the way in. She twisted the doorknob and found it unlocked. She used her foot to open the door slowly. She cringed as the door, probably on one hundred year old hinges, squealed in protest. They certainly weren't going to surprise anyone inside now. The pair stood just outside the door.

"Sheriff. Who is in here?" she called out.

No response.

Alicia stepped just inside the door and used her flashlight to scan the room. It landed on a figure huddled in the corner. The figure whimpered.

Without moving, Alicia questioned her. "Are you Ariel Ford?"

She knew the answer, before the girl responded.

The girl, soaked through, and shivering uncontrollably, looked up into Alicia's eyes. She nodded.

Alicia wanted nothing more than to drop her weapon and flashlight, and run over to the girl and give her a hug. But she knew better.

"Anyone else in here with you?" Alicia glanced around. There was another room, with a closed door.

Ariel shook her head.

Alicia turned to the officer behind her. "Look around."

He didn't have to respond. He went straight for the door. In under twenty seconds, he called, "Clear."

"Go tell everyone outside what is going on in here. Leave us alone. We'll just be a couple of minutes. Go get her a blanket." Alicia realized that she needed to get her medical attention immediately. "And radio for an ambulance."

Alicia knew that having a dozen or so officers suddenly surround her, the girl might clam up. She holstered her gun and walked gently toward Ariel, still huddled in the corner.

"Honey, it's all right. My name is Alicia. I'm here to take you home."

They could hear the excitement brewing outside once the news of finding Ariel alive was given to the rest of the searchers. Alicia ignored them.

Something dark and wet dripped down Ariel's face.

"It looks like you are hurt. Is it okay if I take a look?" Alicia spoke slowly and softly, doing her best to ease into it and make Ariel feel comfortable.

Ariel gave her a slight nod. Alicia lifted her flashlight and shined it on Ariel's forehead, confirming her suspicions that it was blood. Pointing the flashlight higher, Alicia could see a large gash in the area where the girl's hair met the top of her forehead.

The wound appeared deep, but only dripped slowly by that point. It was probably several hours old, at least, Alicia surmised.

Alicia wondered what kind of shape Ariel really was in. She had been missing for five days and may not have had any food during that time. She appeared weak and frail. The girl seemed to be swimming in the jacket she had on.

As they were waiting, Ariel began to whisper something. It was so quiet that she could barely make out what the girl was saying, but Alicia leaned in closer to hear her better. "He's not who you think he is," she told the deputy.

Deputy Alicia Jones' heart sank.

CHAPTER 35

Deputy Jones had concerns that something was off about the man they had suspected all along, but she had hoped she was wrong. He was Ariel's father, after all.

But Ariel's words only confirmed her suspicions. Alicia tried to hide her worry from the young girl, but her face must have betrayed her because Ariel's expression grew even more concerned.

Alicia needed clarification. What if Ariel meant another man. The very one who had been texting the girl for the past several weeks. Or even...Uncle Chris. These were people who were all suspects.

"What do you mean, Ariel?" Alicia asked, trying to keep her voice calm.

"He's dangerous," Ariel whispered, "I overheard him talking to someone on the phone. He was talking about getting rid of us."

Alicia felt a chill run down her spine.

"Who is dangerous? I need you to say it."

The words that came out were almost imperceptible and

Deputy Jones had to lean in closer to catch them. "Can you repeat that?"

"My father," she whispered again.

Alicia had to act fast. She looked around the empty cabin for any signs that Nathan Ford had been there recently. It was getting late, and the darkness only made it harder to see. Jones drew her gun from its holster and checked the magazine to make sure it was fully loaded.

"We need to get you out of here," Alicia said, her voice low and urgent. "Can you walk, Ariel?"

Ariel nodded, her shaky hand reached out for the deputy. Alicia took her hand and helped the girl to her feet. She was definitely unsteady, her knees shaking. Alicia wrapped her left arm around Ariel's waist and guided her out the front door.

Every eye turned toward them as they exited the cabin.

Alicia felt the weight of the stares on them. She knew that keeping everyone out of the cabin would cause her to be scrutinized, judged, and questioned. But right now, she couldn't care less. She had to get Ariel out of there, away from the place where she had been held captive for days.

There was danger nearby. She could feel it in every cell in her body.

Ariel's body shivered as she leaned against Jones. She could sense the fear that was still gripping the young girl, even though they were now outside, away from the danger.

"We're safe now," Alicia whispered, her voice barely audible. "You're safe now."

Ariel didn't say anything, but Alicia could feel her relaxing a bit in her arms. The group of officers parted in front of them, like the Red Sea. Ariel kept her face straight ahead, but slid her eyes left and right, watching the stoic faces next to them.

The pair made their way down the dirt path until they

reached Alicia's car. Ariel stumbled a few times, but the deputy was always there to catch her, to steady her. They walked in silence, the only sounds around them were those of the rustling leaves and an occasional squawk in the night.

The group followed behind, giving them plenty of space in between.

The ambulance hadn't arrived yet, so Alicia opened the passenger door and helped Ariel get in. She buckled her seatbelt and got into the driver's seat.

Alicia started the car and peeled out of the driveway. As they drove away, she couldn't help but feel guilty for not having food in the car for the ailing teenager.

Alicia always kept a couple of fresh bottles of water in her car. She never knew when she would be stuck for hours staking out a suspect.

"Here, drink this."

Ariel took the bottle without question. She drank greedily.

"Whoa, hang on. Don't drink that too fast. It could make you sick."

Ariel pulled the bottle from her lips and looked over at the deputy.

"Small sips, okay?"

Ariel nodded, taking a sip.

"Yeah, like that. We won't be too long. I'm taking you to the hospital to get a check up and get some food into you. Is that okay?"

Ariel nodded again.

The pair rode in mostly silence all the way to the hospital. Deputy Jones wanted nothing more than to ask her question after question about her abduction and what had happened to her in the past five days. But it wasn't quite the time for that.

All that mattered at the moment was that she had been found alive. Everything else could wait.

Alicia contemplated whether to notify Nathan Ford that his daughter had been found, or not. Of course, he would need to be told, but she wanted to get her checked out before that happened.

Was that the right way to go about it? Probably not. At this point in time, Nathan was nothing more than a suspect. He hadn't been found guilty, or even charged with anything. Yet.

And there was always the possibility, though a minute one, that he had nothing to do with the abduction of his children at all. Or even the disappearance of his wife. But all of that seemed such an astronomical coincidence that she brushed it from her mind.

Nathan Ford was guilty. She was sure of it.

CHAPTER 36

A bit more than an hour later, Ariel had been admitted to the hospital, examined, had her head stitched up, and had eaten a few bites of food.

Alicia was by her side the entire time.

Once Ariel had settled in, Alicia leaned forward in her chair, her eyes narrowing as she studied the girl's face. "Did your father take you to that cabin?"

Ariel stared ahead. Alicia wasn't entirely sure that she had heard the question.

"Ariel? Did you hear me?" Alicia placed her hand gently on top of Ariel's. She flinched, retracting her hand, but continued staring straight ahead.

Alicia pulled her hand back to her lap.

"Ariel?" she asked once more. "Please answer me. We need to figure out exactly what happened. It's important, so that nothing like this ever happens again."

"No."

"No, what? No you aren't answering me, or no, your father didn't take you to that cabin?"

"The second one."

"I see. Then how did you get to the cabin?" Alicia was doing her best to keep the story moving forward, now that Ariel was speaking.

"I walked."

Alicia's eyebrows lifted. "That cabin is several miles from your home. You walked the entire way?"

Ariel nodded.

"Why did you walk all the way out to that cabin? Did you go out there all alone? Was Sean ever with you?"

"I needed to get away from my father. I was afraid he was going to kill us."

Alicia sat straight up in her chair. "Us? So Sean was with you?"

"No...I don't know."

"You don't know if Sean was with you or not? What does that mean exactly?"

"He...he was with me, but then...he didn't want to go all that way. He started whining that he wanted to go back home."

"And?" Alicia asked.

"And he did."

"He just turned around and went back toward home, and you let him?"

Ariel shrugged, her eyes sliding over to study Alicia's.

Alicia Jones decided to put that line of questioning aside for the time being.

"Why did you think your father was going to kill you?" Her voice was gentle, but firm.

Those in charge at the sheriff's department had talked while Ariel was being examined. They decided that they would not say anything to her at the moment about her brother being found murdered. Not traumatizing her even more was utmost in their thoughts.

Ariel shifted uncomfortably, her fingers twisting together in her lap. "My dad has been acting strange lately. Saying weird things, like he wants to get rid of us."

"That's what you said back there at the cabin. Do you know exactly what he meant by wanting to get rid of you?" Alicia repeated, her voice incredulous. "Can you explain that?"

Hesitating, it took her a minute to start speaking. "When he noticed that I heard him, he said he was just talking about sending us off to stay with our aunt for a weekend, but...I don't know, something about the way he said it made me feel like he meant something else," Ariel explained, her voice trembling.

Alicia frowned, her mind working quickly to process the information. "Do you have any idea why he would want to get rid of you?"

Again, Ariel hesitated. "I don't know for sure, but I think it has something to do with my mother."

Alicia leaned back in her chair, crossing her arms over her chest. "What about your mother?"

Ariel took a deep breath. "I think he killed my...my... mother." She could barely choke out the words.

"Why do you think that? Did he say something specific to you?"

"No, not really. It was just that all of her stuff was there. She would have taken it. And I don't think she would have left me and Sean and just taken off, you know?"

Alicia knew. Sure, there were certainly mothers who had done that, but that sort of thing was rare. Way more often than not, when a mother went missing, without her children, she was dead. It was just a fact of life.

"He killed my mom, didn't he?" The words coming out of the girl's mouth were low and weak. It was as if by just saying them, it would make them come true.

"We don't know, because we haven't found her body. She might be alive. I'm hoping she is," Alicia told her truthfully. "But Ariel, we just don't know at this point."

Ariel nodded, without responding.

Alicia scribbled something down in her notepad before turning back to Ariel. "Can you think of anything else your father said or did that made you feel uneasy or unsafe?"

"He drinks a lot. And yells at us."

This was not new information to the investigation.

"Tell me about your relationship with your Uncle Chris."

The door to the hospital room burst open. "Where's my baby?!"

Nathan ran to the bed. "Oh Ariel, thank god you're okay!"

Ariel slunk away from him. But there was only so far she could get without falling off the opposite side of the bed, onto the hard tile floor. She grasped the pole to her right that held a bag of something liquid going into her arm. She had no idea what it was…and she didn't care.

Ariel could smell the acrid stink of alcohol on her father's breath. It did succeed in covering up the usual smell of antiseptic and sick people that seemed to permeate every wall of the building.

Ariel hated that smell on her father's breath. It was a constant reminder of his frequent outbursts.

Nathan leaned over and pulled his daughter toward him, bringing her in for a bear hug.

Alicia Jones watched with interest. The look on Ariel's face said it all. She wanted nothing to do with him. That was clear.

Once he released his hold on his daughter, Nathan took a step back and looked at her. Finally, he truly looked at her. He took in her pale face and gaunt cheeks. It was all he could do to not break down in front of her. The entire thing broke his heart.

"I can't tell you how happy I am that at least *you* survived," he told her. "We will never get to see your brother again."

Ariel's eyes widened. "What? What do you mean? Sean is...is...dead?" She could barely get the words out.

CHAPTER 37

"No," Ariel said, her voice raw with grief. "No, it can't be true. Sean can't be dead."

Nathan turned his attention to Deputy Jones, narrowing his eyes at her. He had no idea that they hadn't told Ariel that her brother had been found dead.

"Daddy?" That simple word cut through the room, shattering the silence.

Nathan spun back around to find Ariel clutching a crumpled tissue in her hand, her knuckles turning white from the pressure. Her eyes wide with shock and confusion. The sight of her broke his heart.

"Sweetie," Nathan leaned toward her, wrapping his arms around her tenderly, and kissed her tearstained cheek. "I'm so sorry, baby," he whispered softly. "I'm so sorry."

Ariel pushed him away, her eyes blazing with fury. "Why didn't you tell me?" she demanded, her voice shaking with a strange mixture of anger and pain.

Nathan opened his mouth to speak, but Deputy Jones stepped forward, placing a hand on his shoulder. "We didn't want to upset you until we had more information," she said, her tone gentle.

Ariel's expression twisted with disbelief. "More information? What else could you possibly need to know? My brother is dead!"

Nathan watched helplessly as his daughter crumpled in a heap on the bed, her sobs echoing throughout the room.

It was still hard to believe that his son was really gone, and that they had to break the news to his big sister like this.

As he comforted Ariel, Nathan's mind raced. He couldn't rest until he found out who had done this to his son. He had always suspected that there was the small possibility that he was capable of hurting his children, when he was blackout drunk. Even still…it actually happening seemed so out of character for him. Sober, he would never, not in a million years, ever hurt one of his children. He leaned over and took his daughter into his arms once again. They both needed comforting this time.

"Deputy Jones," Ariel said, as she pushed out of the hug her father had on her. "Can I talk to my dad alone?"

Both Nathan and Ariel watched the deputy as she contemplated how to answer that. She wasn't sure that leaving them alone was such a great idea. But then again, if Nathan really was capable of trying to wipe out his family, would he make an attempt right here in the hospital room, as she stood outside the door? Nah, he wouldn't do that. He couldn't do that, Alicia thought.

"Um, sure. I'll be right outside in the hallway if you need anything."

The pair was silent until the door closed behind the deputy.

The moment she heard the click, Ariel turned to her father. "I need to ask you something and I need the truth. Can you promise me that?"

Nathan gave his daughter a tentative nod.

"Did you kill my mother?" Ariel asked.

The blood drained from Nathan's face, but he kept his words slow and steady. "No Ariel, I didn't kill her. I wouldn't kill her. We had our problems, but I loved her. I still love her."

He averted his eyes, even as he spoke.

"I don't believe you," she told him. "I can never forgive you if you lie to me. If we are going to have any sort of relationship, you have to tell me the truth." The girl crossed her arms and narrowed her eyes at her father.

Nathan studied the ground below his feet. "Maybe." The words were barely a whisper. Tears dribbled down his face.

Ariel's heart raced as that one simple word hit her like a ton of bricks. Her mind was racing, trying to make sense of the situation. Could her own father truly be responsible for her mother's disappearance?

Nathan's tears became heavier, and he shook his head in disbelief. "I...I don't know," he stuttered, his voice laced with guilt and desperation. "I can't remember anything after we fought that night. I woke up the next day and she was gone."

Ariel's heart ached for her father. She could see the pain and confusion etched on his face, and she knew that he was genuinely lost. But the wounds on her head, and the fact that her mother was missing, and probably dead, were too much to ignore.

"You need to tell the police everything you remember," Ariel said firmly, her voice filled with conviction. "They need to find out what happened to Mom. If you really don't remember anything, they can help you figure it out."

Nathan was amazed at the take charge demeanor in his 13 year old daughter. She had always been brave and strong willed, but even that didn't prepare him for the words coming out of her mouth right then.

He took her hand in his. "Am I the one who hurt you?"

Nathan glanced at the wound on Ariel's forehead. "I'm so sorry if I did that. I truly don't remember anything."

Ignoring his apology, Ariel responded. "Just tell the police where my mother is."

He dropped her hand. It plopped onto the hospital bed. "I don't know where she is."

"How am I supposed to believe you?" Ariel pointed at the wound on her forehead and the bruises and scrapes on her arms. "You have hurt us all for a long time."

Nathan lowered his gaze. "I don't know the answers to your questions. I just know that I honestly don't think I had anything to do with hurting any of you."

Ariel narrowed her eyes at her father.

He looked back at her. "And one more thing. I'm going to get some help. I want to stop drinking and be a better father to you."

"It may be too late for that."

Both father and daughter turned toward the voice of Deputy Jones.

"Why?" Nathan asked her.

"Because we are going to do everything we can to prove that you did this." Alicia was not mincing words. And she meant everything she said.

"If I'm going to prison, I should probably start out sober. It'll be easier to do that in rehab first."

CHAPTER 38

Two days later, Nathan Ford walked into a rehab facility, accompanied by his brother, Chris. Though the two of them had a lot of issues between them, those were things they could work on later. Chris just wanted his brother to get the help he needed now to dry out and hopefully remember the events of the last several days.

Cassandra's sister, Desiree, wholeheartedly agreed to let Ariel live with her. At least until Nathan was released from the facility and cleared of any suspicions regarding his wife and children.

Deputy Jones volunteered to pick Ariel up from the hospital. She would take the girl to her house to pick up a few things and meet her aunt there once Desiree got off of work that day.

Alicia walked Ariel to the front door. She used the key Nathan had given her to open it up. "Give me just a minute. I want to do a quick look around, to make sure the house is clear before you go in. Wait for me here, okay?"

Ariel nodded, taking a seat on the front step. She watched the neighbors in their yards and those walking their dogs while she waited. Ariel smiled at the familiar waft of buttered popcorn that always seemed to come from George's house, the old man who live across the street.

The front door opened behind her. "Okay, everything is fine. Come on in."

Alicia held the front door open wide as the girl entered the house. Ariel strolled right in, like nothing had changed, which was very odd to Alicia.

Alicia couldn't blame her if she had been nervous. The last time Ariel was in this house, she was fighting with her father, and her brother was alive. But that wasn't how Ariel looked. Alicia just chalked it up to the fact that different people had different reactions to things.

"Um…Deputy? I'm going to go upstairs and take a shower before Aunt Desiree gets here. I feel really grimy after being in the cabin and the hospital. Is that okay?"

"Sure, honey, that's fine. And you can call me Alicia."

Ariel nodded and hurried up the stairs toward her bedroom.

"I'll just make some tea while you shower and get your things together," Alicia called up the stairs. But the door to the bedroom slammed mid-sentence.

Alicia shrugged and headed to the kitchen.

Finding the tea kettle on the stove top, Alicia carried it over to the sink and filled it up halfway with water. While waiting for it to heat up, she called the office.

"Hey Jake, I'm over at the Ford house with Ariel. She's taking a shower and getting her stuff. I should be back in an hour or so. Any update over there?" she asked Deputy Cavanaugh.

"No, not really. We've questioned some family members again, but nothing new has come up."

"You know, there's something weird about…" Alicia walked to the foot of the stairs and peered up, making sure

145

the girl couldn't hear anything. She could hear the shower running. "About Ariel. She seems way too casual about this whole thing."

"What do you mean?" Jake asked.

"I just mean that I would expect her to seem a lot more traumatized, you know? Like maybe jumpy and quiet. But that's not what I'm seeing at all. She seems like a normal thirteen year old girl. She even smiled when she walked into the house. I just find that weird."

"Everyone reacts to trauma differently. I know that when we found out my mother was the Black River Killer, my sister began acting strangely. Hell, I probably did too. That girl has been through a lot. So it's not surprising that she is out of sorts. Just keep an eye on her. At any point, she could break down. I've seen it happen."

Alicia nodded, even though he couldn't see her. "Yeah, that makes sense. But she hasn't even mentioned her brother once. Not on the ride over, and not since we got here to the house. I tried to bring up the subject, but she didn't respond."

"She could be in shock. Just give her time," Jake advised.

"Yeah, I guess. I just find it odd that she would even want to come into the house after everything that has happened. I don't think I would. I did offer to stop by and get some things for her, but she said she wanted to do it herself. I don't know. Maybe it's just me," Alicia admitted.

"Nah, she's been through a lot. She's the only survivor of a psychopathic father," Jake told her. "It's surprising that she survived at all."

Deputy Alicia Jones gasped.

CHAPTER 39

"Oh my god," Alicia told Jake. "She did this. Ariel set everything up."

There was silence on the other end of the line.

"Jake? Are you there?"

"Yeah, yeah, I'm here," he responded. "I don't think so. No way. She is only thirteen years old. It has to be Nathan. He is the only one capable of everything."

"Maybe. It's just a theory at this point. But if I'm right, this could be really big," Alicia told him.

"Yeah, you could be right. With everything that went on with my own family, I can pretty much believe anything at this point. It does make perfect sense, when I think about it. She hates her father. He's abusive. I don't know why she would hurt her mother or brother though."

"She might not have done anything to her mother. We don't know at this point," Alicia told him. "All of this might just be a coincidence and she really did run off."

"Nah, I find coincidences like that a bit hard to believe. Whoever killed Sean is almost definitely responsible for

Cassandra Ford's disappearance also. I'm sure of it," Jake told her.

"What about the tape we have of Nathan yelling at his kids, and Sean is yelling 'no' in the background?" Alicia asked. "I don't know how to explain that if it wasn't Nathan."

"That would be easy to set up. Nathan did yell at his kids a lot. So all she needed to do was hit record on her phone when it happened, and voila, the perfect set up."

"Wow this is crazy," Alicia responded. "And those nude photos she texted to her uncle could have been a set up also. It definitely put him on our radar."

"Exactly," Jake told her. "And the cabin in the forest. She knew it was there. She knew that we would find her eventually. She hid from everyone in the forest and made it look like she had been hurt and was hiding from her father. None of us suspected a thing, until right now."

"There's no way she bashed herself on the forehead. That was a nasty cut. What do you think? Could it be self-inflicted?" Alicia asked, feeling a bit like she should backtrack on this whole accusing Ariel thing.

"It's easier to do than you think," Jake told her. "My own mother used to do things like that. She liked the attention."

Jake hated nothing more than talking about his psychopathic mother. She had killed dozens of people over a thirty year period and he was caught in the middle of it all. But it seemed important to share some of the details at the moment.

"She took advantage of her father's blackouts," Alicia added. "And the people we talked to about her, they all had good things to say. Wow, if we are right, she is a master manipulator."

"It happens. It's easy for some people to show one face to some people, and be completely different with others. I mean, think about it. Even you are probably a different person with your family, than you are with your friends, out drinking. Am I right?"

"Well yeah...I guess you are," she admitted.

Jake didn't respond. She could sense him nodding across the phone line.

"Jake?"

"Yeah?"

"What if we are wrong? What if her father has been the guilty one all along?" Alicia asked him. "Don't you think we need more than our hunches to go on before we start accusing a young girl of all of these atrocities? Like some actual evidence?"

"So start snooping around," he offered. "You never know what you might find if you try hard enough."

"What if she catches me?" Alicia asked, her eyes darting around the kitchen.

"Just tell her you are looking around for evidence to convict her father. She'll like that answer."

"Okay. I'll call you back in a bit."

Alicia couldn't believe the conversation she had just had. She hung up the phone, feeling a wave of anger wash over her.

Deputy Jones felt a chill run down her spine as she realized the severity of the situation. Was it really possible that this girl had not only staged her brother's disappearance and murder, but she had also orchestrated her mother's disappearance as well? It was likely that Cassandra Ford was also dead. It was clear that Ariel was not as innocent as she had initially seemed.

As she waited for Ariel to finish her shower, Alicia couldn't help but wonder what was going through the girl's mind right now. Did she feel any remorse for what she had done, or was she completely devoid of any emotion?

Was she even right? Or had she just wrongly convinced

herself that a thirteen year old girl was actually capable of killing her mother and brother, and framing her father and uncle of atrocities? Hell...she didn't know. Maybe she was losing her damn mind, and projecting everything onto a poor teenage girl who had just lost her entire family to tragedy.

The whole thing seemed completely absurd when she really thought about it.

When Ariel finally emerged from the bathroom, Alicia couldn't help but notice the girl's calm demeanor. It was almost as if she didn't have a care in the world. She couldn't believe how someone could be so cold and calculating. If that's what she was observing at all.

Her hair still wet from the shower, Ariel headed straight for the kitchen and made herself a cup of tea. When she perched herself on the couch, Alicia didn't know how to react. Something was definitely up with Ariel. Alicia followed her into the living room, and stood watching Ariel sitting casually, sipping on her tea.

It took everything Deputy Jones had to not confront the girl. But she knew that was not going to help. She needed to find some evidence first. Something that Ariel would have a hard time disputing. Her chance came soon enough.

"Ew, this tea sucks."

Ariel plopped the teacup on the coffee table, spilling it over the edge onto the wood. She barely noticed, and didn't care.

"I'm going to go pack."

Alicia watched the girl ascend the stairs toward her bedroom.

CHAPTER 40

Alicia dialed Jake's phone once more. Before he had the chance to say anything, she whispered, "Just hang on. I don't have much time." Alicia stuck her phone, with Jake still on the other line, into her jacket pocket.

She walked to the foot of the stairs, and listened. She heard footsteps and drawers opening and closing.

Satisfied that she had a few minutes, Deputy Jones made a beeline for the garage. She figured that was as good a place as any to start. Maybe later, after Ariel was safely away staying at her aunt's house, Alicia and her team could come back later and search the house. But for the time being, the garage seemed to be the best place to be, since Ariel was in the house.

The garage was in a state of messy organization. One wall held four bikes, all up on hooks and out of the way. Yet, the floor was scattered with a few boxes, a weight pressing bench, and a treadmill, both of which hadn't been utilized in years.

She ran her index finger along the weight bench covering, gouging a long clean trail in the thick layer of dust. She looked at her finger, wiped it on her pants and headed straight for the wall of shelves containing dozens of boxes.

The boxes didn't appear to have been moved in quite some time. When Alicia touched one of them, a cloud of debris wafted in the air, causing her to sneeze.

Most of the boxes were labeled. Some had the kids' names on them, others had objects listed, such as 'photo albums' and 'baby clothes.' But the boxes with no labels on them were the ones Alicia was most interested in.

She pulled one down off the shelf and set it gently on the floor. It was not taped shut, and she opened it with ease. It contained a collection of porcelain dolls. She figured those were being saved for Ariel. Or maybe they had belonged to Cassandra as a child. Or more likely, both scenarios were the case.

The second box was no more interesting than the first. It contained baseball gloves, baseballs, a couple of backpacks, and four tennis rackets. She pushed that box to the side.

Box number three had been shoved all the way to the back of the shelf. Alicia slid it forward and pulled that one down to the floor also. Opening the box made everything come together.

It had a woman's purse, some make-up, some jewelry, and some adult women's clothing in it. Jones pulled out the purse and opened it up. She scanned the room as she did so. The garage was empty and eerily silent. Suddenly she felt as if she were snooping in the neighbor's garage, and had no business being there.

Reaching in, she found a pink wallet and pulled it out. There was no money in it, but the I.D. had the name Cassandra Ford on it.

"What are you doing?"

Alicia Jones let out a little startled squeal and dropped the purse and wallet to the garage floor. She spun around to find

Ariel leaning against the interior garage door frame. How she had gotten the door open without making a sound was beyond the deputy.

"Alicia, I asked you what are you doing?" Ariel repeated.

The deputy cringed at the girl, the one she was pretty sure was a killer, using her first name. Sure, she had told Ariel to call her that. But that was when she was a traumatized child. Not now. Now it was too much. It was familiar. Too familiar. And she wanted nothing to do with Ariel and familiarity. They weren't friends. They were officer and suspect. That was all. That was all they would ever be.

Of course, she hadn't found any evidence that Ariel was the killer. They might be on the completely wrong track. It might still be her father. That was something she needed the answer to.

Alicia Jones took a step back, putting some distance between herself and Ariel. She cleared her throat, trying to regain her composure. "I'm just looking for any evidence that can help us catch the killer," she said, her voice steady despite her nerves.

"And you thought you'd find it in my garage?" Ariel asked.

CHAPTER 41

Deputy Jones shrugged, trying her best to appear nonchalant. "We have to consider every possibility."

Alicia took a deep breath, trying to calm her racing heart. She picked up the pink wallet and held it out for Ariel to see. "While going through these boxes, I found this," she said, trying to keep her tone neutral.

Ariel stepped forward, her eyes trained on the wallet. "Whose is it?" she asked, her voice barely above a whisper.

"Your mother's," Alicia said, watching for any reaction. "Do you know how this got here?"

Ariel's face remained impassive, but Alicia could see a flicker of something in her eyes. Regret, perhaps?

Ariel chuckled, the sound low and throaty. "Well, you won't find anything in there having to do with me, if that's what you are thinking. I'm not stupid enough to leave incriminating evidence around. Besides, who says my father didn't put that stuff in there? You have nothing on me."

Alicia felt a flicker of irritation at Ariel's smugness. She was used to suspects trying to outsmart her, but there was something about Ariel that made her skin crawl. "We'll see about that," she said, bending down to pick up the clothing, most of it still on closet hangers.

"Why would your mother leave and put all of her clothing in a box? Wouldn't she have taken it with her?"

Ariel shrugged. "How would I know?"

Alicia composed herself, ignoring Ariel's question, knowing that it was pointless to answer.

Alicia couldn't help but feel a sense of unease at Ariel's words. She had underestimated the girl, and it could cost her dearly. "I need you to tell me the truth, Ariel. Did you kill your mother?"

Ariel's expression turned cold, and she took a step closer to Alicia. "Why would I tell you anything?"

Ariel's right arm moved to just the right angle, causing the garage light to flash on something shiny the girl held in her hand.

For the first time, Alicia noticed the gun that Ariel held at her side. She hadn't lifted it or pointed it at anyone. Yet. But it was coming. Alicia needed to think quickly.

"Because if you don't, you'll be spending the rest of your life behind bars," Alicia replied firmly.

"Is that a threat?" Ariel challenged, her voice low and dangerous.

"It's the truth," Alicia refused to back down.

A tense silence settled between them, broken only by the sound of their breathing.

Alicia Jones could feel that something was about to happen. She could easily take a 13 year old skinny girl down in a second. But that same girl with a gun? Alicia was no match for that.

Alicia jumped at the vibrating phone in her pocket. Ariel's eyes darted to where the sound was coming from. She pulled the phone out and looked at the screen before Ariel could say a word.

"Oh, it's my daughter. I'll just be a second." She smiled at the young girl, hoping that a sweet call with her 'daughter' would cause Ariel to relax a bit. Maybe she would even set the gun down.

Wishful thinking, she knew.

The thing was, Alicia Jones had no children. It was the office on the other line.

"Hi honey, how are you today?" Alicia said in her sweetest, I'm talking to a four year old, voice.

"It's Cavanaugh," Jake told her, not realizing the ruse. "Sorry about that. We got disconnected."

"I know, honey. I'm kind of busy here with my friend Ariel. I'll be back home soon, okay?" Alicia continued.

"Are you all right?" Jake asked.

"No, not right now. But I can't wait to see you. Soon, okay?" Alicia told him.

"We are on our way." The line went dead.

CHAPTER 42

Alicia Jones stuck the phone back in her pocket and looked up at Ariel. "Little ones. You just gotta love 'em, right?"

Ariel Ford did not answer. Her face revealed nothing. She didn't smile, she didn't frown, she didn't smirk. Alicia could not read her at all.

"All right, Ariel," Alicia continued, trying to keep her voice steady. "We need to talk."

Ariel simply nodded.

"We know that you killed your mother." Alicia said it so matter-of-factly. It was important that Ariel believed it as fact, even if Alicia was not completely sure that it was a fact herself. But this was the time to find out. Showing any signs of weakness could prove to be disastrous.

Ariel shrugged. "So what if I did? Maybe I needed a way to get out of this house." She tilted her head toward the kitchen. "My mother was suffocating me." She let out an exasperated sigh, as if the conversation was of no consequence to her.

The cop felt bile rise in her throat. How could anyone be so callous? Especially someone as young as Ariel Ford.

"We know you recorded your brother screaming for help. You wanted it to seem like he was taken too, so you could make yourself the victim."

Ariel only shrugged at that last revelation.

"How could you kill a little boy? And he was your brother. Doesn't that mean anything to you?"

"I never said that I killed him," Ariel responded, her face devoid of emotion. "You are barking up the wrong tree."

"I don't think we are," Alicia said. "You know your mother loved you, right?"

Ariel shrugged again. "I don't know if she did or not. I do know that she loved Sean more than me. And she was having another baby. She would have loved that one even more. I couldn't let that…"

Ariel's voice trailed off. She realized that she was saying more than she intended. More than she should.

Alicia did the best she could to not reveal her emotions at that moment, and the shock of hearing that Ariel knew Cassandra Ford was pregnant when she went missing. She was positive that was something no one knew about.

So, if that was indeed the case, how did Ariel know?

"I don't remember your father telling us that your mother was expecting a baby when she went missing."

Ariel shook her head. "He didn't know. She told me a couple of days before she disappeared. She said it was our little secret."

Alicia was trying hard to remain composed, but the shock of the revelation was too much for her to handle. She took a deep breath and asked Ariel a question that had been lingering on her mind.

"Ariel, tell me the truth. Did you harm your mother and brother? And did you do it to get back at them for not loving you enough?"

Ariel looked down, and Alicia could see that she was

struggling to keep her emotions in check. After a few moments of silence, Ariel's voice quivered as she spoke.

Ariel replied, her eyes filling with tears. "I just wanted my parents to love me like they loved Sean. But they never did. They always made me feel like I wasn't good enough."

Alicia listened intently, her heart breaking for the young girl sitting in front of her.

"I was so angry about all of it, so hurt."

Alicia's mind raced with possibilities. What if the new baby wasn't Nathan's? The thought made her feel queasy. She pushed it aside and focused on Ariel.

"Why did you think your mother loved Sean more than you?"

Ariel looked away, her hands fidgeting, still holding tightly to the gun. "It was always obvious. She would spend more time with him, buy him better gifts. I was just the afterthought."

Alicia noticed the pain in Ariel's eyes, the hurt that had festered for years. She wondered if that was enough of a motive for Ariel to do something so drastic.

Ariel looked down at her hands, and at the gun. Still, she kept it to her side. "I couldn't let her have another baby," she repeated. "She loved Sean more than me. I couldn't let her love another child more than me too."

Alicia felt like they were on the verge of a breakthrough. Ariel had been dancing around the truth, but still hadn't actually confessed to anything. Maybe now, it all might finally come out.

Alicia Jones stepped forward, her heart pounding with excitement. She was getting closer to the truth. She could feel it. "So you killed her," she said, her voice barely above a whisper.

Ariel didn't answer at first, but then she looked up and

met Alicia's gaze. "I didn't mean to," she replied, her voice trembling.

Deputy Jones' breath caught in her throat. There it was. A confession. But she needed more. She needed the girl to admit to killing her brother also.

Very close to Ariel now, Alicia reached over and patted the girl on the shoulder. "Tell me about Sean. What happened to him? It's important that I know, okay? You can trust me. I'm on your side."

Ariel studied the deputy's face, focusing in on her dark eyes. "I should have cried for him. I guess there's some things I just can't fake."

CHAPTER 43

It took everything Deputy Jones had not to scream. Here she was, standing in front of a cold blooded killer. But the child was only a young teenager. She should be out hanging with her friends, roller skating, or whatever 13 year olds did these days. Not plotting and killing her family. One by one.

Alicia bit her lower lip. She only released it from the vice grip once she tasted that familiar salty, metallic flavor. Without releasing her focus on Ariel, she wiped the blood from her lip with the back of her hand.

Ariel only smiled at the gesture.

Ariel tensed when the cold butt of a gun pressed against the side of her head.

"Drop the weapon," came a male voice from behind the girl.

Ariel dropped it without hesitation.

"Ariel Ford, you are under the arrest for the murders of Cassandra Ford and Sean Ford." Sheriff Garcia turned to Jake Cavanaugh. "Cuff her."

"No, you don't understand. See that cop there," pointing to Deputy Jones. "She has a gun and was going to hurt me."

The crocodile tears didn't fool any of the officers surrounding her.

A few neighbors had emerged from their homes when the police cars arrived. They stood, gawking, as Ariel was led outside. She could see the judgment in their eyes. She dropped her head and stared at her feet as she walked down the sidewalk, hands cuffed behind her back. Her hair was still slightly damp from the shower and it hid her face from prying eyes.

Other than those neighbors watching with interest, no one was there for Ariel Ford that day. She was led to the nearest patrol car and driven to the sheriff's station.

Once she was booked, she was placed in the very interrogation room that her father and uncle had been in just recently.

"Where is your mother?" Sheriff Garcia asked her.

The girl shrugged. "How should I know?"

"Ariel, we heard everything," Sheriff Garcia told her. "We know you killed your mother and brother. So tell me now where your mother is. Let us bring her body home. For your father." His words were soothing. Maybe the gentle approach would work on the girl.

"I want to talk to my dad."

Sheriff Garcia and Deputy Jones looked at each other. That was the last thing they expected Ariel to say. She had made it perfectly clear how she felt about her father.

"Your father is in rehab, Ariel." Alicia spoke first.

"Don't you think I know that?" Her words were calm. "I want to talk to him directly about my mom. He was the one who killed her, you know."

"Why are you lying to us again?" Garcia asked. "I thought we were past this bullshit you are throwing our way."

Ariel looked at Sheriff Garcia with cold, hard eyes. She knew she had to play this carefully if she had any chance of getting what she wanted. She needed to throw them off her trail, just for a little while longer.

"I'm not lying," she said, her voice soft and almost convincing. "My father killed her. He was always angry with her, always fighting with her. It was only a matter of time before he snapped."

Sheriff Garcia looked at her skeptically. "And what about your brother? Did your dad kill him too?"

Ariel hesitated for a moment. She had forgotten about her brother, the poor boy who had been caught in the cross-fire of her father's temper. But she couldn't let them know that. She had to keep up the facade.

"Of course he did," she said, her voice barely above a whisper, her face not betraying her.

Sheriff Garcia shook his head. "Ariel, we have evidence that proves that you were the one who committed these murders. We have witnesses who saw you."

It was a bluff and maybe a dangerous one. Ariel Ford, even at the tender age of 13, was no fool. The sheriff held his breath as he waited for her to respond.

Ariel felt the weight of their accusations crushing down on her. She had thought that she could convince them, but it seemed like they were too set in their beliefs.

"I know what you think," she said quietly. "But my father is the one who did it. He's been abusive for years, and he finally snapped. He killed them and then he made me take the blame."

Alicia Jones scoffed. "That's a convenient story. And I don't believe a word of it."

CHAPTER 44

"Why would I lie about something like that?" she said, her voice low and steady. "You think I killed my own mother and brother for no reason?"

"Then tell us what happened," Garcia said. "Tell us the truth, Ariel. We want to help you."

Ariel took a deep breath, and then another. She'd never told anyone the truth before, not even her best friend. But she needed to tell someone, needed to get it out.

"My father was always drunk." Her voice was barely above a whisper. "He'd come home late at night, yelling and screaming, and hitting my mother. And then he'd leave again, sometimes for days on end. He didn't care about any of us."

"So why kill your mother and brother?" Alicia asked, taking a stab at the fact that it sounded as if Ariel was finally confessing. "It sounds to us like they were victims of your father also."

The deputy's instincts were right.

"I wanted him to suffer," Ariel admitted. "If I had killed him too, he wouldn't be suffering like he is now."

There it was. She finally admitted to killing two members

164

of her own family. As much as Alicia was already positive that Ariel was the culprit, the girl had only danced around the truth. Now it was out in the open.

"Tell me about Sean. What happened? Did he really walk with you that night and turn around to go home? If so, why did you kill him?"

Ariel looked down at her hands for a full minute, before looking back up at the deputy. "Yes, he followed me. I didn't want him to, but he wouldn't listen. I had no choice, I had to kill him. If I hadn't, then he would have ruined everything. He would have told you I was lying about our father, which I'm not. Sean was like that. You couldn't believe anything he said."

Alicia considered the irony in the words coming out of Ariel's mouth. "Go on."

She averted her eyes from the judgmental gaze of Deputy Jones. "So, I did it. I strangled him."

Alicia's heart beat raced as she pictured the poor little boy all alone in the dark, wet forest. "Why just leave him lying in the woods where he could easily be found, instead of burying him?"

Ariel shrugged. "I don't know. I didn't have a shovel with me. And I figured my dad would look more guilty if you knew Sean was dead. If you never found a body, you wouldn't know. Besides, I hated him. He was their golden child. Always was."

Deputy Jones stared at Ariel, trying to process her confession. She couldn't believe that a young girl like her could do something so heinous. She took a deep breath and asked, "Why didn't you go to the police? Why take matters into your own hands?"

Ariel's eyes grew cold, and she replied, "The police wouldn't have done anything. My father is a smart man, and he knows how to manipulate them. I had to do it myself."

Ariel's eyes burned with anger and frustration. "He deserved to suffer," she hissed. "He was a monster. He abused us for years, and nobody did anything to stop him. I couldn't take it anymore."

Deputy Jones felt a pang of sympathy for the young woman sitting across from her. She knew people who had lived with the pain of growing up with abusive parents. But that didn't excuse what she had done.

"You know that doesn't justify murder, right?" she said gently.

Ariel glared at her. "I don't care. I hate him."

Alicia shook her head. "You still should have come to us. We could have protected you."

Ariel scoffed. "Protected me? You weren't there when he was beating me and my mother. You weren't there when he threatened to kill us. I had to protect myself."

Alicia could see the pain in Ariel's eyes, and she softened her tone. "I understand that, but taking someone's life is never the answer. You're going to have to face the consequences of your actions. You know that, right?"

"I'm thirteen. What are they going to do, throw me in jail with adults?" She gave the deputy a sly smile. "Doubtful."

Alicia sighed. She knew the justice system was flawed, especially for minors who committed such serious crimes. But she couldn't let Ariel think that what she did was acceptable.

"Ariel, I understand that you were scared and felt like you had no other choice. But killing someone is never the answer. You will have to face the consequences of your actions."

Alicia leaned in closer to Ariel, her voice low and serious. "You may be young, but that doesn't mean you won't face serious consequences for what you've done. Killing someone is a heavy crime, no matter the circumstances. It's our job to bring justice and keep everyone safe, including you."

Ariel shook her head, her eyes downcast. "I know what I did was wrong. But I couldn't just stand by and let him hurt us anymore. My mother was too scared to leave him, and I was too scared to let him keep hurting her."

Alicia placed a hand on Ariel's shoulder, her expression softening. "I understand why you did what you did, but it's not up to us to take matters into our own hands. That's why we have laws and a justice system in place. I'll do my best to ensure you're treated fairly, but you need to cooperate with us and tell us everything. You need to take this seriously, Ariel. You took a life. Two lives actually. Regardless of your reasoning, there will be consequences."

Ariel's smile faded, and she looked down at her hands. "I know," she said softly. "But what else could I have done? He was going to kill us."

Alicia sighed, feeling a pang of sympathy for the young girl. "I understand that, Ariel. And I'm not saying that you didn't have the right to defend yourself. But taking a life is a very serious thing."

Ariel nodded, tears beginning to well up in her eyes. "I know," she said again. "I didn't want to do it. I didn't want to hurt anyone."

Alicia leaned forward, placing a gentle hand on Ariel's shoulder. "I believe you," she said softly. "But now you will need to face what you have done."

CHAPTER 45

The door to the interrogation room burst open with the power of a gale force wind. Both Alicia and Ariel Ford jumped in response.

"Where is your mother, Ariel?" Sheriff Garcia demanded.

Ariel looked down at her feet.

Garcia was losing patience with the teen. "We don't have time for this. Answer me!"

"Okay, okay. She's in the woods, near where you found Sean. She's buried between the big rocks. But I didn't put her there."

Sheriff Garcia locked eyes with Deputy Jones, who just shook her head.

"Really?" he asked. "Then please enlighten me as to who did put her there."

"My father."

"I don't believe you," he told her outright. "I already know that you admitted to killing your mother and your brother."

"I lied."

"And why would you do that?" Garcia prodded.

Ariel shrugged. "I don't know. I just felt like it, I guess."

"Young lady, stop playing games with us." Garcia spoke through gritted teeth.

Sheriff Manuel Garcia was an understanding man. He was a patient man. At least he thought so. Ask some of his co-workers and that may not be what they report. But he didn't care. He knew what type of man he was. But this 13 year old girl was trying every last nerve in his body. It was all he could do to not throw her into a holding cell until her hair turned gray and her body withered from old age.

Obviously he couldn't do that. He had no authority as far as sentencing her. All he could do was investigate her crimes and hope with everything he had that she would be convicted and sent to a detention center for as long as humanly possible.

He had heard of other cases where kids were convicted and got sentences lasting decades. They were older, as far as he knew, more like 16 or so. But it didn't matter. She was a killer. Two homicides and she had barely started her teen years. She needed to be off the streets. No matter what.

And he would do everything in his power to make sure that happened.

"I'm not playing games," the girl replied, interrupting his thoughts. "My father made me help him bury her. Then he told me he would do the same to me if I ever said anything. I'm afraid of him."

"Then why tell us about it now? Aren't you still afraid of him?" Garcia asked her.

"Maybe. I just don't remember for sure what happened. You can't prove who did it. I know that and you know that. My father has been abusing us for years. You all are stupid if you don't think it was him."

The left side of her mouth curled up into just the slightest of smiles.

Sheriff Garcia watched her. She kept eye contact, she didn't flinch. She was a monster in the making.

After several seconds, he turned and walked out of the room without another word.

CHAPTER 46

"Ah geez," Sheriff Garcia said, almost under his breath. His face blanched and his stomach lurched. But he managed to stand his ground.

Sheriff Garcia, along with Deputies Jones and Cavanaugh, stood over the haphazard gravesite, deep in the woods. It was exactly where Ariel Ford said it would be. Boulders flanked the site.

The bones appeared to be of an adult female. Everyone was sure it was poor Cassandra Ford lying before them. But tests would have to be done to verify it.

"That girl is unhinged," the sheriff added, leaning back against the nearest boulder, doing his ever best to keep his last meal down.

"We still don't know for a fact that it was her," Jake Cavanaugh told the pair.

Garcia and Jones looked at him with wide eyes.

"Are you kidding me?" the sheriff asked. "She admitted it, and she pointed us right to her mother's body. How can you possibly question her guilt?"

"Yes, I'm well aware that she pretty much said she did it.

But then she backtracked and said it was her father. I'm just not convinced it was her," Jake replied. "I think she has a lot of problems, and maybe she was even emotionally and physically abused. She might not actually know for sure who killed them, even if she is the one. I've seen it before."

"Jake, I'm with the sheriff here," Alicia replied. "I know she took her story back, but she did that a bunch. First she didn't do it, then she did, then she can't remember. It was her. We all know that."

"Well, I don't know that." Jake's words were curt. "She needs help, that I'm sure of. But this..." His arm swept across the air over the bones lying before them. "This is beyond comprehension. I just don't see a girl her age being mentally, and physically, able to carry out something like this. I mean, am I crazy here?"

Sheriff Garcia lifted his eyes to the dark sky and watched a black cloud practically fly across in the swift wind. He turned to Jake. "Yeah, you might be. Or maybe not. Hell, I don't know. It could be either one of them, I guess."

Pulling away from the boulder that had kept him upright, now that he was feeling just a bit better, Garcia spoke directly to his deputies. "It's cold out here. I'm going in." He turned to the excavation crew, who were carefully removing the dirt around the skeleton. "Get the body to the coroner right away. We need absolute confirmation of the identity."

"You two," speaking to Jones and Cavanaugh, "go to the rehab center and have a talk with Nathan Ford. I'm tired of this cat and mouse game. We need to know for sure who did this. And don't come back till you have an answer. And the right one."

CHAPTER 47

Jake watched as the sheriff retreated back to his car, the headlights illuminating the impending dark, enclosing forest. The wind picked up, sending a chill down his spine. He couldn't shake the feeling that they were missing a crucial piece of the puzzle, or perhaps, there was just something off about this case.

He turned to his partner, Alicia Jones, who was studying the excavation crew as they worked. "What do you think?" he asked her.

She shrugged. "Now that I think more about this, I might be coming around, Jake. Something here doesn't add up."

"Alicia, I want you to do me a favor," he said, his voice low.

"Anything. What do you need?"

"I want us to come back here, once these techs are done, and comb through all of it one more time. We need to look for anything that might have been missed. Anything at all."

Alicia nodded, understanding the gravity of the situation. "Of course. We'll get on it right away. Whatever it takes to get to the truth."

They both knew that the rehab center was their next stop. Nathan Ford was the key to unlocking this case. He had been admitted to the center shortly after his daughter had been found.

Jake nodded before climbing into the passenger seat of the car. They drove in silence for a few minutes before he spoke up.

"You really think it was her, don't you?"

Jake kept his eyes forward as he spoke. He wasn't sure he could keep it all in if he looked directly at his partner. This case had brought up so much of his own history with the Black River Killer.

Alicia Jones shook her head. "Honestly, I just don't know anymore. One minute I'm convinced it's her. The next, I'm convinced that her father did it. We definitely still have a lot of work to do to figure this one out."

Jake and Alicia arrived at the rehab center and were led to Nathan's room by a nurse. The woman was pushing 70, and walked with a slight limp. Her orange scrubs were a bit too tight around the middle, and she seemed uncomfortable, pulling at the fabric as they walked. The long hallway seemed to take forever at the nurse's pace. Jake let out a frustrated breath, but never said a word.

She pointed at the door of room number 41 and stepped aside as they walked in. She followed.

As they entered, they saw the man lying on a bed, his eyes closed and his breathing shallow. The pair watched him. In only a few days, he looked pale and like he had lost a good amount of weight.

"I don't think he is going to be of much help to you. He's

been sedated," the nurse said, before turning on her heels and leaving the two of them alone with Nathan.

Jake spoke up first. "Mr. Ford?"

Nathan didn't even stir.

"Mr. Ford? Can you hear me?" His words were a bit louder this time.

Jake walked over to the bed and stared down at the man below him. He looked dead. But Jake could just make out the rise and fall of Nathan's chest. He reached down and gently shook Nathan's shoulder. Still nothing. There was no indication that Nathan was aware at all of anyone in his room.

Shaking him with a bit more gusto this time, Nathan stirred, but never opened his eyes. "Whaa?"

"Mr. Ford, can you hear me?" Jake asked again.

Nathan took a deep breath. "Mmmm hmmm." He opened his eyes into the narrowest of slits. It took a few moments before recognition dawned. "Oh you." His words were mumbly. "What do you want?"

"We need the truth from you, and we need it now." Jake was not mincing words. The sternness came through in his voice.

Alicia side eyed Jake and jumped in before things got out of hand. "What we mean is, we would like to speak with you about your daughter."

"Hmmm, oh, um...Ariel? What about her? Is she all right? She's not d...d..." He rubbed his forehead with his right palm. "I can't bring myself to say it. I can't lose anyone else."

"No, Mr. Ford," Alicia replied. "She's not dead."

A cleansing breath escaped the father's lips.

"Where is my Ariel?"

"She's at the sheriff's station. She's perfectly fine," Jake told him, keeping his voice calm and even this time.

Alicia approved.

"Why do you want to talk to me about her then?" Nathan

175

spoke as he slowly sat up in the bed and swung his legs over the side, touching the cold, bare concrete below. He barely noticed. His daughter, the only person in his family left, was the only thing he cared about at the moment.

"She's been telling us about you," Alicia replied. "About how you have been abusing all of them. For several years."

"What? That's not true."

Jones hesitated for a moment. "Well, if that didn't happen, then I think the only reasonable explanation for all of this is that your thirteen year old daughter is a cold blooded killer. She killed your wife and strangled her own brother. Is that what you are trying to tell us?"

Nathan didn't respond.

"Or is what Ariel is saying the truth, and you have been an abusive asshole all these years?"

Nathan's eyes grew wide. "My daughter would never say that."

"Let's go," Jake announced, heading toward the door. "He's not going to be of any help to us at the moment."

"Wait."

CHAPTER 48

Deputies Jones and Cavanaugh gave each other a look. It had worked. Nathan Ford was about to confess to everything. He was going to tell them that it was true, he had been abusive. He had killed Cassandra. He had killed Sean. It was the moment they had all been waiting for.

Nathan looked the deputies square in the eyes. He didn't flinch. He didn't look away.

"Ariel is a liar."

Alicia and Jake looked at each other again. That was the last thing they expected to hear. A father throwing his own daughter under the bus.

Jake spoke up first. "We don't believe you."

"It's true. Ariel is making all of this up. I've suspected Ariel of hurting her mother for a while now." Nathan couldn't quite yet bring himself to say the word 'killed.'

"Really? And why is that?" Alicia asked him.

"She has just been acting strangely ever since Cassandra's disappearance. At first, I chalked it up to missing her mother. But after a while, there were little things. Like she would speak about her mother in the past tense, and make comments as if she was never coming back."

"Can you elaborate on that?" Alicia asked.

He thought for a moment and let out a breath. "Well, let's see. She once said something like, 'Now that Mom is gone, can I have her jewelry?' You know, stuff like that. Then I would say that her mother might want that back one day. She said that she wouldn't. We would never see her again. Just stuff like that. It happened a lot."

"But what possible motive could your daughter, at only about twelve at the time, have to kill her own mother?"

"I wish I knew the answer to that. The truth is that she has always been a bit...different."

Alicia tilted her head. "In what way?"

"She just..." Nathan thought for a moment. "She just doesn't seem to have empathy for others. You know, like when her brother fell on his bike and broke his wrist. She didn't care. Just...nothing. Like it was of no consequence to her."

"Yeah, but," Jake answered, "that doesn't sound so unusual for brothers and sisters. Does it?"

Nathan shrugged. "I don't know. Maybe that was a bad example. It doesn't really matter who it is. She doesn't seem to care one way or another if someone is hurt, or crying, or even worried about something. It's like nothing is of any consequence to her. She just doesn't care."

"And you say she has always been this way?" Jake asked.

"Yeah, pretty much. I even remember once when she was in Kindergarten, she bit another girl on the face. We sat her down and tried to explain why that was wrong. She didn't seem to get it. And then she did it again to another kid not long after. She has done that sort of thing to numerous kids over the years. Each time, we tried talking to her about it, but got nowhere. She just didn't seem to get what the problem was."

"So Ariel is the liar?" Alicia asked.

"That's what I said."

"This whole story seems a bit farfetched to me," Alicia added.

Nathan placed his left hand on his stomach and grimaced. "Can I get something to eat and drink? I'm feeling a bit nauseous."

Jake indicated the door with just a tilt of his head. "Come on, let's go."

Once outside of the rehab center, Jake stopped and turned to his partner. "Look Alicia, I know you know the history of my mother's...um crimes."

Alicia nodded.

"She was just a small child when she started her decades long killing spree. So, I'm not saying what Nathan Ford said was true, but it certainly is possible for a child to commit those crimes. You get that, right?"

Alicia took a deep breath and let it out slowly. "Of course I get that. But not everyone is your mother." She hadn't intended on the words sounding so rough. "Nathan Ford could very well be lying. But you know what...I don't think he is. I think Ariel Ford is exactly what he was dancing around. A killer. And a remorseless one at that."

CHAPTER 49

The excavation crew had left and the area was silent, except for the wind moving dried leaves about. Jake walked around the site, closely examining the ground, the dirt and rocks crunching under his feet. Studying the ground intently, his eyes caught something glinting in the dirt. He knelt down to take a closer look.

Jake's heart began to race as he realized what he had found.

"Hey, can you get a pic of this?" He motioned to Alicia, not touching the item, as he placed a latex glove on his right hand.

"Whatcha got there?" Alicia asked, pulling her phone out of her pocket and kneeling down to get in close. The object was very small. She pulled back the phone to get better focus. "Oh." She and Jake locked eyes, without speaking.

Once Alicia was finished, Jake reached down and picked up the small silver earring. He held it up like a trophy between the two of them.

"Do you remember that photo of Cassandra Ford wearing

these exact earrings on her social media profile? If I'm not mistaken, I am pretty sure this is one of them."

Alicia searched her memories for just a moment. "Oh yeah. You are right." She got in closer to the earring. "I think this is the same one. I can't believe you remembered that."

"We've only found this one earring here. I have a good idea where the twin to this one might be." He dangled the earring like some sort of prize.

"Where?" Alicia asked.

"In Ariel Ford's jewelry box."

"Oh no."

Jake knew what he had to do. He called the sheriff and the coroner, informing them of the new evidence.

Within minutes, Sheriff Garcia and another deputy drove straight to the Ford house.

The pounding on the front door startled Desiree, causing her to jump and drop the plate she had been hand drying. It shattered into tiny bits across the kitchen floor. She stared at it without moving. "Great. More work. That's just what I need."

The pounding on the door, once again made her jump. "What the hell?" She threw the dish cloth that she had been clinging to in her hand onto the top of the shattered dish, and headed for the front door.

The pounding started once again just as she pulled it open. She caught Sheriff Garcia with his fists mid-air.

Desiree gasped. "What is going on?"

"We need to come in," the sheriff told her. It wasn't a request.

She stepped back and held the door open wider. "Of course. What is this all about?"

Without stopping to have a chat, he headed down the narrow hallway and called over his shoulder, "We need to check Ariel's jewelry box."

Desiree followed on their heels. "Yeah, I guess that's fine. What are you looking for?"

"Her mother's earring."

"Her mother's..." Desiree couldn't finish her sentence. She stopped short at the entrance to the hallway, her feet unable to move.

Equipped with the photo that Alicia Jones had taken less than an hour prior, the sheriff fished the earring out of the jewelry box and held it up next to his phone.

It was a perfect match.

CHAPTER 50

ONE YEAR AGO

"Ariel, where's your dad and your…?"

Cassandra Ford found herself staring down the business end of a gun. She gasped. "Ariel…wha what are you doing with that? Where did you get that gun?"

"Get in the car. We are going for a ride," 12 year old Ariel replied.

"What is going on here? Ariel, put that gun down now. You might hurt somebody."

The girl indicated the front door of their house with a flick of the gun she was holding. "Go. Now."

"Ariel, stop right now. What do you think you are doing?"

"We are going on a little road trip. Now let's go, before I shoot you between the eyes right where you are standing."

Cassandra looked her eldest child in the eyes. Ariel wasn't there. Not her sweet pre-teen girl, who loved to cuddle on the couch on Saturday nights and watch silly comedies with her parents. Not the girl who seemed to adore her mother, following her around, asking questions about make-up and boys. What was happening?

Cassandra was perplexed at this sudden hatred that she saw in her daughter's eyes. It was as if Ariel was no longer in there. Her soul had been ripped from her body, and the person who stood in front of her was no longer her daughter.

"Ariel, I don't understand what is happening. Where did you get that gun?" Tears dribbled down the face of Cassandra Ford.

"Shut up and move."

Cassandra did as she was told. Maybe during their drive she could talk some sense into her daughter.

"Go that way," Ariel indicated a left turn. "When you get to that dirt road by that old lady's house, you know the one, turn right."

Cassandra knew the one.

"Okay, now I've turned. Why are we heading down this road? Why are we going into the forest?"

"Just keep driving." Ariel's eyes never left her mother, as she leaned her back against the passenger door and held the gun aimed squarely at her face.

Ignoring her daughter's tone, she continued. "Ariel, where are we going?" Cassandra struggled to control the car as they drove down the rutted dirt road that wound its way through the forest. Her body shook and her teeth rattled from the constant bumps and grooves in the road.

"I said keep driving."

At this point, Cassandra was terrified. She didn't recognize her own daughter.

"You always loved Sean more than me."

Not daring to take her eyes off of the road, for fear of hitting a rock, a tree, or even a darting critter, Cassandra spoke softly. "That's not true, honey. I love you both the same."

"Liar!"

"Honey, I'm not lying. Why would you think that I love him more?" Her heart was breaking for her child that felt unloved, even for a moment in time. And she was telling the truth. In Cassandra's mind, her children were both deeply important to her. She couldn't imagine loving one more than the other.

"You are nicer to him."

Cassandra thought about that declaration for a moment. Was it true? Maybe. Ariel, as sweet as she sometimes was, could be trying at even the best of times. She had hit that pre-teen attitude with full force. The girl was cranky and argumentative. Nothing ever seemed to make her happy. And picking on her little brother seemed to have become her favorite pastime.

Against her better judgment, Cassandra responded with a question. "Don't you think that you have some responsibility in that? I mean, your attitude with all of us has been pretty bad lately. Wouldn't you agree?" She knew it was confrontational, but felt it might help to get her daughter to face her own failings in the family.

"I don't have an attitude."

"Yeah, okay," Cassandra said under her breath.

"Stop here."

Cassandra applied light pressure to the brakes and came to a full stop. "Now what?"

"Get out."

CHAPTER 51

"Honey it's dark and cold out there. Can't we just talk in here?"

Ariel lowered her head and looked up at her mother with the coldest of eyes. Cassandra involuntarily shuddered. She raised her hands up, palms facing her daughter. "Okay, okay. I'm getting out."

"Leave the engine running."

Ariel climbed out and walked around to the front of the car. She motioned for her mother to join her. Cassandra's silver earrings glinted off of the headlights.

"Go over there, by those boulders."

Cassandra did as she was told. She glanced over her shoulder as she walked toward the darkness.

"What are you doing, honey? I don't understand any of this. I love you. You know that, right?"Cassandra couldn't control the shivering that seemed to reverberate throughout her body.

Ariel did not respond.

Cassandra stopped dead in her tracks and stared down at

the grave sized hole in the ground. Her head snapped up to get answers from her daughter.

"What the...?

"I hate you, you know that, right?"

She didn't know why it took her so long, but Cassandra finally realized that her daughter was unhinged. She blamed herself. Maybe she had treated Ariel differently. Maybe she did prefer her son. Sean was such a sweet boy, and Ariel... well, she could be...difficult.

"Why do you hate me? You have to know that I love you. I've always loved you."

"I don't believe you. You ignore me, and Daddy yells at me."

"Your dad..."

Ariel interrupted her mother mid-sentence. "At least Daddy pays some attention to me. But not you. You only care about your precious little boy."

"Honey, that's not..."

"Don't call me that! I'm not your honey. I hate you!"

"We can work this out. If you'll just put that gun down, we can talk. I want to talk. We can go over there and sit in the car all night if you like, and work this out. I just need you to put that gun down." Cassandra wanted nothing more than to keep her eyes on the gun, but she didn't dare pull them from Ariel's deadly gaze.

"I'm not going to go sit in the car with you all night. You aren't leaving these woods."

Cassandra wrapped her arms in front of her waist and rubbed them. Summer or not, it got quite chilly in the forest at night. She considered the ramifications of what her daughter had just told her. She wasn't leaving these woods. Could her own child, her own flesh and blood, actually shoot her and leave her in a hole in the cold dark forest? Was that something a 12 year old child would even be capable of doing?

Cassandra stepped toward her daughter and opened her arms. "Honey, please. I…"

The shot that rang out echoed off of the trees and seemed to disappear somewhere deep into the forest. An owl screeched and flew off at the sudden explosion of sound coming from below him.

The hot, tearing feeling in her chest seemed to happen before she even registered the sound of the gunshot. Cassandra looked at her daughter with wide eyes, not really comprehending what had just happened. There was no expression on her daughter's face. It was as if shooting her own mother was just another day to her.

When the second gunshot rang out, Cassandra registered that one immediately. It hit her squarely in the heart, causing her to lose consciousness within a couple of seconds. Her knees buckled and she tumbled into the hole that Ariel had managed to dig over the past several weeks.

Ariel walked over and looked down into her mother's grave. She didn't care that the woman who had given birth to her was dead. It was of no consequence to her.

Something on the ground glinted in the car's headlights. Ariel looked down to find one of the silver earrings that her mother had been wearing when she was shot. She picked it up and pulled her hand back to chuck it into the hole, along with the dead woman. Just before releasing it, she hesitated. Instead, she stuffed it into her pocket and smiled. It was her own little souvenir.

One last glance and she walked around one of the boulders next to the grave and grabbed the shovel she had left there.

～

Once done with her task, she walked at least a quarter mile into the forest and dumped the shovel into a deep ravine, figuring no one would ever find it. And if they did, they would have no clue where it came from.

Luckily for Ariel, her father had taken her and her brother out a handful of times and let them drive the car, just for fun. It was always out on forest roads, where they wouldn't hurt anyone if they lost control. Ariel had turned out to be surprisingly good at it.

She drove the car home, carefully, and on backstreets only. They really didn't live far, so she had no problem getting home without incident.

Finding her father passed out drunk in front of the living room TV was exactly what she had expected. He had no clue that she had even left the house. Ariel smiled to herself.

CHAPTER 52

Nathan Ford's eyes involuntarily squinted in the bright sunlight of the morning that he finally walked out of rehab.

He was a free man. At last.

"Hey man." Chris was leaning back against Nathan's dark green car.

During his weeks in rehab, Nathan had forgiven his brother for the affair with Cassandra. He had already lost his wife, his son, and now his daughter. Chris was all he had left.

Because Ariel was so young, the District Attorney decided to not advocate for prison. Instead, she would spend the next few years in a psychiatric facility. At least until her eighteenth birthday. At that point, her case would be reviewed, along with her progress, and a decision would be made about her future as a resident in the facility.

Nathan Ford agreed with the psychiatrist's assessment that she stay there. He loved his daughter, nothing would ever change that. She was still his baby girl. But after what she had done, he wasn't sure if he could ever forgive her, and he couldn't bring himself to visit her. Maybe that would change in a year or two, maybe not. But definitely not right now.

Nathan had a lot of time to think while he was in rehab. His life was going to change. He would make sure of that. He would never touch alcohol or drugs again. He was sure of that. It wouldn't be easy, but he would make it work.

Now that his body was clean and free from everything he had been doing to it, the next thing he needed to do was clean up the rest of his life. He put his home up for sale. He needed a fresh start, away from death, away from his daughter, away from all of his demons.

Taping up the last of the boxes, Nathan was deep in thought, wondering what this new chapter of his life would bring.

"How are you doing, Mr. Ford?"

Nathan jumped at the sound, turning around to find the deputy standing before him.

"Hello, Deputy Jones. I wasn't expecting you."

"I'm sorry I startled you. The door was open."

Nathan shrugged. "It's fine. I'm just about done here anyway."

Her eyes scanned the room. "You moving?"

Nathan nodded. "I've lost my entire family, Deputy. It's time that I moved on with my life. It's really all I can do, don't you think?"

Yeah, Alicia thought. She couldn't blame the man. He had been through hell and back.

"Where are you going?"

"Oh, one of my old friends from college has a rental house in a small town outside of Seattle. He said I could stay there as long as I wanted." He shrugged. "I figured I could use a change of pace, and it'll do for now."

"What about your daughter?"

Nathan took in a deep breath and let it out slowly, before answering. It was a question he had heard more times than he could count over the last few weeks.

"You know, after everything that happened, I no longer have a daughter. I'm leaving her, and all of this behind. And, no offense, but I never want to see the town of Black River again."

Have you read the Ivy Mystery Series? It's time travel with a twist.

THE MANY LIVES OF IVY WELLS
by Michelle Files

Ivy Wells never wanted to die. When she does, she thinks it's all over. It isn't.

When the 30 year old mother of two wakes up as a 12 year old, she has to navigate her life all over again. And she remembers everything, including the serial killer who is terrorizing her small town.

Ivy Mystery Series:
    The Many Lives of Ivy Wells - Book 1
    The Many Lives of Sam Wells - Book 2
    The Many Lives of Jack Wells - Book 3
    The Many Lives of Georgie Wells - Book 4

Author Note

Thank you for reading my book. As an author, your support is extremely important. If you liked this book, please leave a great review on the site you purchased it from. And please consider reading one of my other titles. :-)

If you enjoyed this book and would like information on new releases, sign up for my newsletter here:

www.MichelleFiles.com
Thank you!

www.ingramcontent.com/pod-product-compliance
Lightning Source LLC
Chambersburg PA
CBHW051253250626
47155CB00009B/3288